Murder in the Pearl District

A Cedar Bay Cozy Mystery - Book 5

BY

DIANNE HARMAN

Published by: Dianne Harman
www.dianneharman.com

Interior, cover design and website by
Vivek Rajan Vivek
www.vivekrajanvivek.com

This is a work of fiction. Names, characters, places, and incidents either are the product of the author's imagination or are used fictitiously, and any resemblance to actual persons, living or dead, business establishments, events, or locales, is entirely coincidental.

ISBN: 978-1511711104

CONTENTS

	Acknowledgments	i
1	Chapter One	1
2	Chapter Two	6
3	Chapter Three	12
4	Chapter Four	15
5	Chapter Five	20
6	Chapter Six	24
7	Chapter Seven	27
8	Chapter Eight	32
9	Chapter Nine	37
10	Chapter Ten	43
11	Chapter Eleven	48
12	Chapter Twelve	52
13	Chapter Thirteen	56
14	Chapter Fourteen	60
15	Chapter Fifteen	65
16	Chapter Sixteen	72
17	Chapter Seventeen	76
18	Chapter Eighteen	81
19	Chapter Nineteen	88

20	Chapter Twenty	93
21	Chapter Twenty-One	99
22	Chapter Twenty-Two	104
23	Chapter Twenty-Three	107
24	Chapter Twenty-Four	111
25	Chapter Twenty-Five	115
26	Chapter Twenty-Six	122
27	Chapter Twenty-Seven	125
28	Epilogue	129
29	Recipes	133
30	About Dianne	140

ACKNOWLEDGMENTS

I want to thank you, my readers, for making my books so popular. This is the fifth book in the Cedar Bay Cozy Mystery series, and I hope you'll enjoy it as much as you have the others. It really pleases me that so many of you have taken the time to email me with your thoughts about the books and letting me know how much you like them. Again, many thanks! If you have time, a review is always appreciated. As always, I'd love to hear from you about this book or any of the others. Here's my email address: dianne@dianneharman.com.

One of the things I hear from my readers is how much they like the book covers and I couldn't agree more. I have Vivek Rajan to thank for creating them. I not only think of him as my editor, formatter, and marketing guru, I think of him as a friend.

Finally, all of this has been made possible because of the support and love of my family and particularly my husband, Tom. He believed in me from the start and has become such an integral part of the process, I can't imagine doing it without him. And to Kelly, my puppy, thanks for messing up the manuscripts by putting your paws on the computer keyboard when you wanted attention!

CHAPTER ONE

Kelly looked at the screen on her ringing cell phone and recognized the name "Sophie Marchant."

"Sophie, what a pleasant surprise. How are you doing?"

"Much better than the last time we talked. I've gotten over Jesse's death and the fact that my beautiful home in Cedar Bay burned down. It took me awhile after Jesse's death, but I decided I couldn't live the life of a grieving woman any longer, so I've developed a rather active social life. As a matter of fact that's the reason I'm calling you," she said in her soft French accent. "A friend of mine who is a well-known chef is filming her first television show in three days here in Portland. I'm giving her a celebration dinner party in two days, but my caterer just called me and cancelled. Apparently she got the flu from her children, and she's quite ill. Normally I would cook the meal myself, but since I'm the hostess and I've invited twenty people, I don't think I should. I know it's short notice, but I'm hoping you can come to Portland and cook the meal I've planned for my guests."

"Wow! I'm honored, but I don't know if I'm good enough to cook for a chef."

"Of course you are, *chérie*. You own Kelly's Koffee Shop, one of the best places to eat along the Oregon Coast. Jesse told me that whenever tourists ate at your coffee shop, they always wanted to come back again. Jesse was always talking about what a great cook you are."

"Well, thank you, but in my mind there's a difference between a chef and a cook, and I've never considered myself to be a chef. And to cook for a chef who is the guest of honor? I don't know, but I must say I'm intrigued. What's the chef's name?"

"Donatella DeLuca."

Kelly was quiet for a moment and then she said, "Good grief, Sophie. Everyone's heard of her. She's about the hottest chef around. I have several of her cookbooks, and I refer to them all the time. They're wonderful. How do you know her?"

"Her home is next to an old warehouse building I own which I have converted into my home. We kept bumping into each other at various places here in the Pearl District where I live, and I started eating at her wonderful restaurant called Mangia! Mangia! We became friends, actually, very good friends."

"I'm sorry, Sophie, but I don't think there's enough time. I'd have to drive to Portland, we'd have to decide on a menu, and then I'd have to buy the food. Timewise, I don't see how it could possibly work out. The logistics seem insurmountable."

"Kelly, I've already bought all of the food. The caterer and I decided on a menu a long time ago, and even though Donatella is Italian, I'll be serving a classic French dinner. The recipes are my personal ones. All you'll have to do is drive up here to Portland, and then do your magic in the kitchen. A lot of the food can be made in advance, and of course I'll help. Plus, I have plenty of room, so you can stay with me, and I seem to remember you have a boxer dog. I think I mentioned to you that my dog, Amelie, is a boxer too. Why don't you bring yours? Amelie gets lonesome, and I think they'd be able to play together and have a good time."

"You're making this hard for me to say no. I've always wanted an excuse to explore Portland's Pearl District. From what I hear, it's kind of an urban island of eclectic shops and people located not far from the downtown Portland area. I'll tell you what. Let me make a couple of phone calls and see if I can get Roxie to manage the coffee shop for me while I'm gone, and of course I'll have to make sure it's okay with Mike if I leave for a few days. I'll call you back in a little while."

"I'll be waiting for your call, *chérie.*"

"Hi, Roxie. It's Kelly. Sorry to bother you after hours, but I just got a call from Sophie Marchant. You may remember that she was the woman from Portland who was romantically involved with Jesse prior to his murder. Anyway, she was planning a big dinner party for a friend when her caterer had to cancel because she became ill. Sophie has asked me to come to Portland and prepare the meal. I'd be gone a couple of days and was wondering if you could cover for me. I know you have some friends who helped out at our wedding reception. Maybe one of them could help you, and of course Madison will also be there."

"No problem, Kelly. You deserve a couple of days off, and Portland's a fun place to go. Sure, I'm happy to do it, although I don't know if the regulars will be able to get through their day without a dose of Kelly."

"Actually, Roxie, I've always thought they come to see you, so that shouldn't be a problem. You know where I keep the emergency key. Just use it, and if you have any problems, give me a call."

"The coffee shop and I will be fine. Enjoy yourself."

"Thanks. See you in a couple of days."

She pushed Mike's office number into her telephone and caught a glimpse of herself in the mirror. The reflection was that of a woman in her early 50's with jet black hair secured at the back of her head by a tortoiseshell clip and large sea-green eyes. She was dressed in her customary uniform of jeans and a red T-shirt. When she was working at the coffee shop, she added a white apron with the words "Kelly's Koffee Shop" embroidered on it in large red letters.

Well, one down, now for Mike. I kind of remember him saying something recently about his sheriff's office being really busy right now. Maybe it would be a good time for me to go. "Hi, sweetheart. I had a call from Sophie Marchant a little while ago." She told him about the dinner party that Sophie had asked her to prepare and cook.

"Absolutely, Kelly. Rebel, Lady, and I will be fine. You said she lives in the Pearl District, and I know you've always wanted to explore it. Stay an extra day or so. We'll get by, but I do have one request."

"Sure, what?"

"You know that caramel sauce I love? Would you make a batch of it, and I can have it over ice cream when you're gone? It's one of my favorite things, and it's been way too long since you last made it."

"Happy to do it, but Mike, Sophie specifically asked that I bring Rebel with me. She has a female boxer and thought it would be good for her dog to have another dog to play with. Is that a problem?"

"Of course not. Lady can come to work with me, and you can take Rebel with you. Actually, I'll feel better knowing he's with you. Lady's a good guard dog, but I still think Rebel's the best. Nothing is going to happen to you with that dog around."

"Mike, I'm simply going to Portland to cook a dinner for a chef. What could possibly happen to me?" she asked innocently.

"I don't know, but you seem to attract interesting situations that usually result in a problem."

"Don't be silly. I promise I'll be fine."

Later, she wished she'd never made that promise to Mike or at least she wished she'd mentally crossed her fingers behind her back when she made it. She couldn't help it that interesting things that resulted in unusual problems often happened when she was involved and unfortunately, those unusual problems always seemed to involve murder.

CHAPTER TWO

As she was driving to Portland early the next morning, Kelly had second thoughts about agreeing to help Sophie with the dinner party. She'd spent some time the evening before looking at the cookbooks Donatella had written as well as articles about her posted on the Internet. It didn't help Kelly's level of comfort to read that the Governor had asked Donatella to cook an anniversary dinner for he and his wife.

She was the toast of the town and the darling of the people who lived in Portland and loved good food. Her reputation had evidently spread elsewhere in the United States as her restaurant, Mangia! Mangia!, was recognized nationally as the best Italian restaurant in the Portland area. The only other restaurant which received accolades like that was the Thai restaurant, Pok Pok. Given these factors, Kelly had grave concerns that she was in way over her head.

Interesting, Kelly thought as she drove past the rolling green hills and lush green forests of coastal Oregon, *I looked her up on the Internet, read pages of newspaper articles about her and thoroughly examined some of her cookbooks that I own, but I couldn't find one bit of personal information about her. I wonder if she's married, how old she is, or if she has children. Strange there wouldn't be some little glimmer of information about her personal life.*

The only things I saw that were even halfway personal were the numerous photographs of her. She wears her jet black hair short, and it frames what looks like a very pretty face. She has an olive complexion with dark brown eyes which she accents, and from what I saw, she has a very voluptuous figure that's probably seen its fair share of pasta. Actually, she looks like a younger version of the Italian movie star that was so popular years ago, Sophia Loren. You sure would think there was a man somewhere in the picture, but none was mentioned.

"Okay, Rebel, we're almost there. That looks like Sophie's building at the end of the street. She told me to park in the underground lot." Kelly drove down the ramp that led to the basement parking lot and turned the engine off. "Let's go." Rebel jumped out of the back seat while Kelly got her travel bag from the rear of her minivan. They took the elevator up to the first floor where it opened into a small room with a door on the far side. Sophie had told her to ring the bell next to the door when she arrived.

"*Chérie*, Amelie and I are so glad you're here," Sophie said as she opened the door. She was every bit as chic as Kelly remembered. Brown hair that had been highlighted framed a porcelain complexion and accented brown eyes with thick lashes. She wore a cream-colored silk blouse and slacks with a diamond drop on a thick gold chain around her neck. Matching earrings completed the outfit.

A beautiful female boxer dog walked across the room and sat next to Sophie. She had white stocking feet, a blaze of white on her chest, around her neck, and continuing up her face to form a diamond. Rebel walked over to Amelie and sat down beside her.

Of course Sophie would have a beautiful elegant dog. Why am I not surprised?

"Welcome to my home. I hope you and Rebel will enjoy your stay. I made the first floor of my building into my living quarters, because I wanted a yard with grass for Amelie, even though it's quite small. Rebel, Amelie, come." She walked over to the sliding glass door that led to the back yard and opened it for the dogs. "They can play out there for a while. Please follow me, and I'll show you to your room. It's the one on the left at the end of the hall."

Kelly looked around in awe as she followed Sophie down the hall.

Similar to Sophie's home in Cedar Bay, everywhere Kelly looked there was a piece of furniture or a decorative art object or a painting that was absolutely breathtaking. Although Sophie's home in Portland had a different feel from the home she had on the cliff in Cedar Bay, this home was just as beautiful as the one that had been destroyed in an arson-caused fire.

Lighted cabinets housed brilliantly colored art glass. Paintings that hung on the walls were each illuminated with a soft spotlight. The walls and carpeting were a pale ivory color that tastefully accented the artworks that were neatly arranged everywhere Kelly looked. Sophie had obviously traveled the world. Her eclectic taste ranged from Oriental carpets which covered the floors in all of the rooms to cut glass vases with blooming flowers in all shades of the rainbow spilling out of them. It was a feast for the senses.

Sophie opened the door of the bedroom where Kelly would be staying and said, "There's a bathroom through that door and a sitting room with a computer and a television through the other door. I put a large dog bed at the foot of the bed for Rebel. If you need anything else, please let me know."

"Sophie, this is absolutely beautiful. How many people live in your building?"

"Like so many apartments and condominiums in the Pearl District, this was an old warehouse which I renovated. There are three floors above mine with two apartments on each floor. I have tenants living in those apartments. Donatella lives next door in a house between my building and a building similar to mine on the other side. This kind of architectural mishmash is quite common here in the Pearl District. You know, a little of this and a little of that.

"To change the subject, I thought this afternoon we could look at the menu for the dinner party and maybe even prepare a few things that we will be serving tomorrow night. I want to take you to Donatella's restaurant, Mangia! Mangia! for dinner tonight. It's just across the street. That's what I love about the Pearl District. Everything I need is within walking distance. The only thing I don't like is the traffic on the street in front of my building. Fortunately, Amelie is very well trained, so I don't have to worry about her getting hit by a car. And Rebel? Is he trained as well?"

"Yes. That won't be a problem."

"Why don't you make yourself comfortable, and when you're ready please join me in the kitchen for lunch. We can talk about the menu for tomorrow night then." She left and walked down the hall to the kitchen, her high heels clicking on the highly polished wooden floor.

Kelly looked at the large king size bed with the pineapple patterned quilt. She remembered a conversation she'd had many years earlier with her daughter Julia about pineapples and how they were often viewed as a sign of hospitality. Julia had told her that according to legend, when the sea captains of New England, who sailed among the Caribbean Islands, returned to their home port with cargos of fruits, spices, and rum, they would spear a pineapple on a fence post outside their home to let their friends know of their safe return. It was an invitation for their friends to partake of the food and drink the sea captain had brought back from his travels. She wondered if Sophie knew about the legend or simply liked the beautiful pattern on the quilt. Kelly decided to treat it as a sign of hospitality.

"Ah, there you are. This is a rather late lunch, but I thought you should have something after your long drive and Mangia! Mangia! does serve a lot of food, so I don't think we should eat too much. Please, have a seat. The dogs are enjoying the sunny day in the back yard, and we can feed them before we leave."

"Sophie, I hardly think seafood crepes in a white sauce qualifies as a simple lunch! My mouth is watering just looking at them. I can't believe how beautifully you've garnished the tops of the crepes with more of the crab and shrimp, and this salad is simply gorgeous. It looks like everything in it was picked only a few minutes ago."

Sophie smiled sheepishly. "It was. I have a large raised vegetable garden in the back yard. That was another reason I wanted to live on the ground floor."

Kelly took a bite of one of the seafood crepes and tasted the delicately seasoned mushrooms along with the crab and shrimp. "Sophie, if this is any indication, I really think you should be preparing the dinner tomorrow night. I had no idea you were such an accomplished cook. No wonder you and Donatella are good friends."

"If fewer people were coming, I probably would, but I'm really thankful you could come and help. Here's what the caterer and I decided on." She handed Kelly a sheet of paper with the menu written on it.

Kelly spent a few minutes studying it and then looked at Sophie. "This sounds wonderful, and I think you were very wise not to try and compete with Donatella by preparing a traditional Italian meal. A platter of several kinds of cheese with nuts and fruit is a perfect appetizer and everyone loves baguettes. We can slice them right before we serve it. French onion soup is always a welcome addition to a meal, a salad from your garden, coq au vin, and although you have chocolate mousse listed for dessert, may I suggest something different?"

"Of course. What are you thinking of? By the way, although I have the ingredients for everything else, I do need to go to the bakery tomorrow and get fresh baguettes, so I can get whatever you need."

"The dinner is fairly rich with the French onion soup with its crusted crouton and cheese topping and also the coq au vin, the French dish of chicken and vegetables that's swimming in a rich gravy type of sauce. I noticed you have a lime tree in your yard, and I saw there were a number of limes on it. I have a recipe for a terrific frozen key lime pie that's very light, and I think it would be a nice way to end the meal. Would that be all right with you?"

"Absolutely. Let me know what you need for it, and I'll pick it up when I get the baguettes."

"I'll nose around your kitchen this afternoon while we're getting ready. You probably have everything, but I want to double check. Other than the limes, I'm sure your kitchen has pretty much all the standard ingredients I'll need."

"Perfect. Let's get started."

CHAPTER THREE

Kelly and Sophie spent the next several hours setting the table, arranging the glasses, and selecting various different wines which they placed on the sideboard, making decisions about timing, serving, and all of the other things that go into hosting a successful dinner party.

"Kelly, don't worry about doing the dishes tomorrow night. I'd like you to join us when you can. I have someone coming in early the day after tomorrow to clean up everything. I want you to just walk away from the inevitable mess that will be in the kitchen."

"I'd love to meet your guests, but I'll have to see how it goes. It's been my experience that if anything can go wrong in the kitchen, it probably will. Having said that I'll make a promise to you, I'll do my best to make sure you and Donatella enjoy your special evening. Speaking of her, I'm very curious about Donatella. I looked her up on the Internet and browsed through several cookbooks she's written, but I didn't find any personal information about her. Being a close friend of hers, I'd love for you to tell me a little about her."

Sophie was quiet for a moment, evidently deciding how much she should tell Kelly about Donatella. Finally she spoke, "Dede, that's what her close friends call her, is a very private person and with good reason. She was married to a man she loved very much, but he couldn't handle her success and divorced her. He married a woman who is very happy to have the man in the relationship be the center of attention.

"After the divorce, Dede borrowed heavily to finance Mangia! Mangia!, and it's become enormously successfully." Sophie took a deep breath and continued, "The tragedy of Dede's life is that her daughter by her ex-husband suffers from a severe developmental disability. She will never be able to live by herself or attend a regular school. Francesca is fourteen now, but unfortunately she only has the mind of a three year-old. It is a very sad situation. Her ex-husband has remained a good father to Francesca, taking her a day or two a week, but he can't afford to help with the round the clock nursing care and other things Francesca requires. She's a very sweet little girl with the body of a young woman but the mind of a small child." She shook her head from side to side with a sad and forlorn look on her face.

"Francesca is absolutely the single most important thing in Dede's life. That is why she works so hard. She has to pay for all the special care Francesca requires and believe me, caring for her is enormously expensive. She does not want anyone to know about Francesca and guards her daughter's private life like a mother lioness."

"Well, that certainly explains why I couldn't find out anything about her. From the photos I saw, Donatella is quite beautiful. Is there presently a man in her life?"

"Yes. She has been seeing Mitch Ramos for a year or so. You'll meet him tomorrow night. He's the owner of the television station that is producing Dede's show, Dining with Donatella. I like him, and I think their relationship has become quite serious. She told me he's the first man who has shown a willingness to accept Francesca for what she is. That characteristic is extremely important to Dede. I've never had children, but I can certainly understand her feelings."

"Something you said interests me. The man she is seeing is the one who owns the television station which will produce her new program. How lucky for her!"

"Yes," Sophie said, "She had never thought about having a

television program even though it seems like there's a cooking show being broadcast every time you turn on the television. When people found out Mitch was seeing Dede, they suggested he hire her to do a cooking show. That's how it all came about. Some people think the reason that Dede started seeing him was so she could get her own cooking show, but that simply is not true. Chef Pierre DuBois, who owns Le Toque restaurant, has been telling anyone who will listen that he was the first one to approach Mitch about a cooking show, but Mitch turned him down and instead, gave the show to Dede."

"I'm not familiar with his name. Is he a well-known chef in the area?"

"Yes, certainly here in Portland. Obviously he is French, and he is a very good chef. I think the reason Mitch didn't have him do the show is that Pierre is very pompous, and the people who know him well, even his own staff, don't like him. I hear he has a very bad temper and is a very jealous person."

"Well, I'm sure Donatella's show will be a huge success, and thanks for telling me about her daughter. My heart goes out to any parent who has to struggle with raising a child that suffers from a severe handicap. I'm really looking forward to meeting her."

"You will love her. Everyone does. Her staff idolizes her, and she has fans all over the world. I'm honored to call her my friend."

"She's probably just as honored to have you host this celebration dinner. I'll make sure to do you proud."

"Kelly, I never doubted it. That's why I wanted you and no one else to rescue me when my caterer cancelled on me."

CHAPTER FOUR

"I hope you don't mind, Kelly, but I always let Amelie have the run of the house when I'm gone. I have a good security system, but I think she's far better than it is."

"Rebel will be fine doing the same. One look at those two dogs, and anyone who might be thinking about entering this house would back out as fast as they could. I'll be ready to go once I feed him and let him out."

It was a warm August evening in Portland as dusk slowly turned to darkness. The streets were filled with people taking part in the "Gallery Art Walk," a monthly event when the art galleries in the Pearl District stayed open until 10:00 and served wine and cheese to the gallery guests. It had become a very important night to the art community with many of the galleries making the majority of their monthly sales on those nights.

As they crossed the street, Kelly saw the words "Mangia! Mangia!" written in bold gold letters on a canopy over the entrance to Donatella's Italian restaurant. "Mrs. Marchant, I'm so glad you're able to join us tonight," the handsome young Italian doorman said.

"I couldn't ask a friend of mine to come to Portland without treating her to dinner at Mangia! Mangia! You know it's my favorite restaurant."

"Mrs. DeLuca is in her office. I know she'll want to see you."

"Thanks, Tony. I'll tell Carlotta to let her know I'm here."

As soon as they walked into the restaurant a beautiful young Italian woman greeted Sophie. "It's good to see you, Mrs. Marchant. Please, follow me. I saved your usual table for you."

"Thank you, Carlotta. I'd like you to meet a friend of mine, Kelly Reynolds. This is her first time here."

"In that case we definitely want to make her dining experience with us unforgettable. We'll try even harder than usual," Carlotta said, gesturing towards a table located along the far back wall of the restaurant. As she handed them menus, she said laughingly, "Mrs. Marchant, I'm probably wasting this menu on you. I'm sure you could recite it forwards and backwards."

"I'm sure I could, but even so, I still like to look at it. Every time I come here I promise myself that I will order something new and different, but I never do."

"Enjoy. Stefano will be your waiter tonight. Ah, here he is. I'll check back with you later, and I'll let Mrs. DeLuca know you've arrived."

When Stefano had left after taking their wine order, Kelly said, "I'm dying of curiosity. What do you usually order? It all looks so very, very good."

"I think you will find that everything on the menu is wonderful. Even though I always order the same thing, I have been known to take a bite or two off of my dinner partner's plate, but done so purely in the name of research," she said laughing. "I can't get past the stuffed squash blossoms, clam linguini, the vegetable platter, and for desert, tiramisu. I know the traditional Italian meal has five courses with a main course following the pasta course, but my stomach simply can't take in that much food. I've learned this is perfect for me. And what looks good to you?"

"I'm going to have the bruschetta with sautéed mushrooms and clam linguine. If the vegetable platter will feed two, I can share it with you, and I'm also going to have the tiramisu."

"You won't be disappointed, I promise." She looked up at Stefano as he placed their wine glasses on the table and they gave him their orders. "Thank you, Stefano."

Kelly looked around the restaurant and found it hard not to compare the warm inviting brick walls, the gleaming silverware, and the crisp white tablecloths to her small coffee shop with wood siding located on the pier that jutted out into Cedar Bay. While fine art from the local galleries in the Pearl District graced the walls of Mangia! Mangia!, in her coffee shop the only things gracing the walls were historical photographs of the city's past. Fresh flowers in crystal vases had been placed on each table in the restaurant and the soft light given off by the candles on each table made every woman beautiful and every man handsome.

Even with all of this, I still have a better feeling for my coffee shop and the people who come there. I know them all, and I deeply care about them. They're like family to me. From the looks of the people in here, they probably wouldn't feel at home and enjoy Kelly's Koffee Shop. Their loss. I have to admit that while this is lovely, I'm homesick for Kelly's Koffee Shop.

They were halfway through the antipasto when a beautiful dark-haired woman who Kelly recognized from her photos as Donatella DeLuca approached their table. "Sophie, how good to see you." Sophie stood up and they exchanged the traditional European cheek kisses. Donatella turned to Kelly. "You must be Kelly Reynolds. Sophie speaks so highly of you, and I appreciate your coming to Portland to help Sophie out. I'm really looking forward to tomorrow's dinner," she said in a soft voice with a noticeable Italian accent.

"Mrs. DeLuca, it's a pleasure to meet you," Kelly said, extending her hand. "I'm one of your biggest fans. I have all of your cookbooks and use them frequently in my coffee shop. I realize my little coffee shop in Cedar Bay is nothing like this large and beautiful restaurant, but many of your recipes have found their way onto my menu."

"Good food is good food no matter where it is served. I would love to stay and talk, but I'm having a few issues in the kitchen that require my attention. *Buon appetito,* and I'll see you at 6:00 tomorrow evening."

"I can't imagine trying to run a restaurant like this. I know how much it requires just to run my coffee shop. Not only is this much bigger, but I don't have to deal with fine dining, wine, and a large number of employees. I'm sure there are also guests who probably consider themselves to be far more important than the ones I serve in our small town."

"Yes, that is true. Dede has told me just when she gets the kitchen help all working as a team, there will be a problem with a supplier or a guest or someone who has had too much wine and needs to feel important by finding fault with a bartender or server. She said it's always something, and yet even with all of that, there is very little turnover among her staff. I recognize almost everyone, and I believe that says something about the owner."

They ate the rest of their dinner and talked of this and that. The busboy had just cleared their table when Stefano placed a limoncello drink in front of each of them. "Compliments of Mrs. DeLuca. This is a digestif drink that is traditionally served after an Italian meal. It is Mrs. DeLuca's favorite."

"Thank you. It looks wonderful. And I must tell you the clam linguine was probably the best I have ever had," Kelly said. When Stefano had left the table she said, "Sophie, I need to use the restroom. Where would I find it?"

"It's down that hall past the kitchen. At the end take a right. You can't miss it."

Kelly stood up and began walking down the hall. When she was halfway down it, she heard raised voices coming from behind the door that led to the kitchen. She recognized Donatella's voice speaking in an obviously angry tone of voice. "I don't care what you think. That is not how I want that dish cooked. I will not have my dishes changed or altered in any way, shape, or form. If you want to stay on as sous chef in my restaurant, you will cook the dishes exactly as I tell you, not how you think they should be cooked. Do you understand what I'm saying?"

"Is that a threat? Are you telling me that if I don't cook something your way, you'll fire me?"

"Take it however you want, but I will tell you this, if you want to continue your position as the sous chef at Mangia! Mangia! you will cook every dish exactly as I want it cooked. I don't want to have this discussion again." Her voice faded as she evidently walked away.

Kelly then heard the muffled words *"Ti odio"* angrily repeated several times by the person who had been speaking with Donatella. She had no idea what the words meant, but from the man's tone of voice, she knew they weren't words of love or friendship. Although Sophie had told her everyone loved Donatella, from what she had just overheard it seemed like there was one person who didn't.

CHAPTER FIVE

The next day flew by for Kelly and Sophie, both intent on making the upcoming dinner party for Donatella a success. As the hour of 6:00 approached, Kelly put the finishing touches on the cheese platters, while Sophie changed clothes and prepared to greet her guests.

Three hours later, Kelly removed the frozen key lime pie dessert plates from the dining room table, stacked the dishes for the kitchen help Sophie had hired to clean up in the morning, and put the last of the food away. As she walked into the dining room, she was met with a round of applause. Stunned, she looked at Sophie. "Please, Kelly, join us. I introduced you to everyone earlier, but we want you to know how wonderful the dinner was. I speak for everybody when I say thank you."

Donatella stood up. "Kelly, that was one of the finest meals I've ever had." She turned to the other guests, "Please join me in toasting Kelly Reynolds. I know I speak for all of us when I say I wished we lived closer to Cedar Bay so we could eat at Kelly's Koffee Shop. Now I see why Sophie spoke so highly of you and was so confident that you could fill in for her caterer. Thank you for making this one of the best nights of my life!"

A handsome man with greying temples was seated next to Donatella. Sophie had introduced him to Kelly earlier in the evening. He was Mitch Ramos, the owner of the television station and the man Sophie had mentioned was very close with Donatella. He stood up and raised his glass. "I would be remiss if I didn't toast the woman everyone in the United States will be talking about after tomorrow's television debut of Dining with Donatella. I know I speak for all of us when I say how excited we are for the inaugural show." He turned to Donatella, "Dede, here in American show business there is an expression that means 'do well.' We say 'break a leg,' and that's what we all wish for you, metaphorically speaking. I know the show will even surpass the amazingly favorable media buzz it's already received. And now I think it's time to end this evening. I don't want the star of the show to have bags under her eyes from staying out too late. Ladies, gentlemen, I think it's time to leave."

When the last guest had left, Sophie turned to Kelly and said, "I can never thank you enough. Everyone had a wonderful time, and the food was incredible. You really are a very talented cook, and your frozen key lime pie was a perfect way to end the dinner."

"Oh, thank you, Sophie. I've never done anything quite like this. You never told me specifically where the recipes came from. They really were good."

Sophie smiled sheepishly. "I told you they were mine, *cherié,* and each one was created by me. I love to cook, but I've never had the confidence to prepare and serve a meal to a large group of friends. I like to experiment when I'm cooking for myself. I pretend I'm cooking for a large number of people and they love my food. I know, it's *très* silly, but it's my little secret."

"Well, if you ever want to cook for a crowd of people, you'll always have a job at Kelly's Koffee Shop. Those were excellent recipes, plus what I liked about them was they were fairly simple. I'm sure everyone thought each item on the menu had been slaved over for hours. Very well done."

"*Merci.* You must be very tired, I know I am. Dede invited us to be her guests at the filming tomorrow at 10:00 in the morning. After that I thought we would spend a little time in the Pearl District, exploring. You mentioned on the phone that you had always wanted to see it. I hope you'll spend tomorrow night here at my home and then go back to Cedar Bay the next day."

"I'd very much like that. I've never been in a television studio, and it will be particularly exciting since I know the star. She must be very hard-working. Mitch wanted to walk her home, but I overheard her tell him she needed to check in at the restaurant before she went home. Does she have night care for her daughter as well as day care in her home?"

"Yes, although she told me her ex-husband had taken Francesca for a few days, and she had given Francesca's night nurse and day nurse a couple of days off. I imagine she wants to be rested and calm when she does the show tomorrow, and Francesca can be a bit of a handful at times. Good night. Sleep well."

"I will. I need to call Mike and tell him how the dinner went. He was concerned, and I also need to tell him I'm staying over an extra day. See you in the morning."

After Kelly and Rebel walked into her bedroom, she closed the door and picked up her phone. "Hi, Mike. I know you're probably getting ready for bed, but I wanted to fill you in on the party." She proceeded to tell him all about the menu and the guests.

"Sweetheart, I never doubted you could pull it off. If you lived in a big town, you'd probably own the best restaurant there. Tell me about Donatella."

"I liked her when I met her last night, and she was just as gracious tonight. I guess the tragedy of her life is that she has a severely mentally challenged daughter she shields from the public and the press. Sophie told me she has to work very hard to make enough money to pay for her daughter's expenses because her ex-husband just barely gets by financially. One thing was kind of interesting. Sophie had said how much everyone loves Donatella, and certainly from what I saw, that's true, but I did overhear something strange last night when I was at her restaurant and was making my way to the ladies restroom." She told Mike about the heated exchange she had overheard between Donatella and her sous chef.

"Kelly, are you sure he said, *'ti odio?'* I have a good friend who's Italian, and if that's what you heard, he sure doesn't like Donatella. It means 'I hate you' in Italian. Could you have misunderstood the words?"

"I don't think so. They sounded pretty clear to me, and he sounded very angry."

"Well, no one's perfect, and I imagine Donatella isn't either. Have a wonderful time tomorrow, and I'll see you day after tomorrow. How's Rebel doing?"

"Getting spoiled. Sophie's never had children, and I think her dog, Amelie, is taking a child's place in her life. Do you know what she fed the dogs for dinner tonight?"

"No, what?"

"Filet mignon. Can you believe it? I don't know if we'll ever get Rebel to eat plain old dry dog food out of a bag again."

Mike laughed. "Well, everyone needs to feel a little spoiled once in a while. It won't hurt him, and I'm sure he's loving it."

"Oh yeah. I used to kiddingly get mad at Doc when he fed Rebel a piece of steak as a treat, but a whole filet mignon? Unbelievable. I guess some people have more money than they know what to do with, but Sophie could not have been more gracious to me. Love you, Sheriff. See you soon!"

"Sleep well, Kelly, and give Rebel a big belly rub for me."

CHAPTER SIX

"Good morning Kelly, I hope you were able to sleep after doing so much work yesterday," Sophie said, looking up from her morning newspaper as Kelly walked into the kitchen and poured herself a cup of coffee.

"I don't know when I've slept so well, and you know what was even better, I didn't have to get up before dawn and go to the coffee shop. I feel positively decadent."

"Well, I'm glad you're awake and refreshed. I was going to knock on your door in a few minutes, because we need to be at the television studio by 9:30 and it's already 8:00." Just then Sophie's cell phone began to ring, and she walked over to the counter to answer it. "This is Sophie Marchant." She listened for a moment and then said, "Yes, Mitch, I have a key to her house. She was supposed to be at the studio at 7:30, and she hasn't shown up? That's very strange. Dede is almost fanatical about being on time. I'll go over there now and call you back in a few minutes."

"Kelly, I have to go over to Dede's house and see if she's still at home. Maybe there's been an incident with Francesca. I'm sure there's a logical reason why she's not yet at the studio. I keep her key in my bedroom. I'll be back in a minute."

"I'll go with you. I could use the exercise, and it looks like a beautiful morning. Actually I think I'll take Rebel. He could also use some exercise after his filet mignon dinner last night."

"If Rebel's going, Amelie will want to go too."

A few minutes later, the two dogs, along with Kelly and Sophie, walked next door to Donatella's house. "Sophie," Kelly said, as they opened the gate and began walking up the sidewalk to the porch, "her house is absolutely beautiful. It looks like it's been here since Portland was founded."

"It has. Her house is a good example of the oddities we have here in the Pearl District. This is a strange area. Originally it was considered kind of like what I think you call 'the wrong side of the tracks' with its light industry, warehouses, railroad yards, and a few scattered homes in between. In the mid-1980's it went through a period of urban renewal, and now it has everything from the world famous Powell's City of Books to art galleries and dog parks. A lot of the warehouses were renovated and converted into lofts and condominiums. As you know, my building is one of those.

"I love it here. The area draws people who are quite individualistic. You don't see the, what do they call them? The suits? You know, men dressed in dark suits with vests who work in prestigious businesses. Come to think of it, I can't remember ever seeing a woman who lives in the Pearl District carrying a designer logo bag. Maybe that's why I love it. It reminds me of France. The people here are oh so very interesting. What's also interesting is that it's named after a woman. A man who revered her mentioned this area as being Pearl's District when he was being interviewed by a magazine. The story was picked up by a number of other magazines and the name stuck."

"How charming. I didn't know that."

They walked up the steps to the front porch and Sophie knocked on the door. There was no answer. She rang the bell and knocked again. Still, there was no answer. She turned to Kelly, "I really don't like to do this. Dede is a very private person, and I'm not sure she'll be happy about me taking the liberty of walking into her house, but I'm afraid I have no choice." She put the key in the lock and opened the door.

Immediately a low rumbling growl came from Rebel. Every hair along his spine was erect, hackles clearly raised. "Rebel, easy," Kelly said. "Something must be wrong, Sophie. I trust Rebel. I've seen him do this before when there's danger. We better be careful. Rebel, come." She stepped into the eerily quiet house.

"Dede, are you here? It's Sophie and Kelly," Sophie called out. There was no answer. They walked down the hall, looking first into the dining room and then the living room. There was no sign of Donatella, and everything appeared to be in its proper place.

As they approached the rear of the house and started to walk into the kitchen, Rebel began snarling and barking, standing as close as he could get to Kelly. Almost immediately Sophie screamed, "*Mon Dieu*," and at the same moment Kelly saw Donatella lying face down on the kitchen floor in a pool of blood, a large stainless steel chef's knife protruding out of her back, shining in the morning sunlight which filled the room. She was wearing the same dress she'd had on at the dinner party the evening before and was obviously dead.

CHAPTER SEVEN

Kelly and Sophie both stared in disbelief at the dead body of Donatella, unwilling to believe what their eyes were telling them. Donatella, the vibrant and famous chef, ready to film her first television program, Dining with Donatella, had been murdered in the kitchen of her own home. In an ironic twist of fate, the weapon that had been used to end her life was a chef's knife.

"I'll call the police. Did you bring your phone?" Kelly asked.

"*Non*, I thought I'd only be gone a minute. I can't believe this. I think I'm going to be sick."

"Sit down. I see a phone on the desk. Take some deep breaths. It will pass." She dialed 911.

A few minutes later, they heard police sirens getting louder the closer they got to Donatella's home. Kelly hurried to the front door and waved the police in. "She's in the kitchen at the end of the hall."

When they reached the kitchen, Sophie was crying and trying to talk on the phone. "Mitch... it's Dede. She's ddddead. There's a knife in her back." She handed the phone to Kelly, "I ccaan't talk."

"Mitch, this is Kelly. I am so sorry to have to tell you this, but Donatella has been murdered. Sophie and I discovered her body on the kitchen floor of her home just minutes ago. The police just got here." She listened for a moment. "I understand. You're right. There's nothing you could do here, anyway. I'm sure you'll have your hands full at the station. We'll call you later."

They spent the next hour telling the police and a man who wore a badge with the words "Detective Masters" on it, everything they knew about Donatella and the events of the evening before. The coroner came, officially pronounced Donatella dead, and then took her body to the morgue. Neighbors and the lunch staff from the restaurant filled the front yard, trying to find out what had happened to their beloved chef. The police put yellow tape around the house as detectives and other law enforcement personnel swarmed around the scene of the murder.

Finally, Detective Masters closed his notebook. "You're free to go. I have your contact information if we need to get in touch with you. If you think of something, please call me, no matter how trivial you think it might be." He put his hand on Sophie's shoulder. "I'm sorry. My wife has all of her cookbooks, and I know she was a large donor to a number of charities in the Pearl District. You're not the only one who will feel this loss."

Kelly and Sophie walked back to Sophie's house, the dogs following them. "How fast life can change," Sophie said in a terribly sad voice. "When I got up this morning, I was so happy about how well last night had gone and looking forward to watching the taping of Dede's first show. Now…" her words trailed off as she started quietly sobbing.

"I haven't had near enough caffeine to deal with this," Kelly said. "I'm going to make another pot of coffee. Would you like some?"

"*Oui*. I can't believe this. Because of her diminished mental capacity, Francesca won't understand, and what will happen to her now?"

"Surely Donatella must have provided for Francesca in her will. Do you think Francesca's father can care for her? Will his new wife be able to handle it?"

"I don't know. I've not met either one of them. I imagine Detective Masters will tell him. I gave the detective her ex-husband's name, and I'm sure they will find his phone number in the house. I don't have it."

They each sat quietly at the kitchen table for a few moments, trying to think of a reason why someone would want to kill the popular chef.

"Kelly, I have no right to ask this of you. Actually, I'm going to ask two things of you. First of all, the restaurant needs to stay open. If it closes for even one night, that will be like a death knell for it. I'm wondering if you would run it for the next few days."

"You're kidding, right? I've never worked in a large restaurant, much less overseen it. I'm sure the sous chef could handle it."

"No. Dede was having some kind of trouble with him. She recently mentioned to me that he wanted to do things his own way, and he and Dede had argued about it. Please, just for a few days. I'm sure your Sheriff Mike would understand, and it would provide a little extra time to get Francesca situated and let people know nothing is going to change at the restaurant."

"Well, I've never done anything like this, but I have to say I'm intrigued. Tell you what. If Mike doesn't have an objection, I could probably stay for a few days. Of course, that's also contingent on making sure it will be all right with Roxie, who's managing Kelly's Koffee Shop for me while I'm gone. You said you were going to ask two things of me. What's the other thing?"

Sophie took a deep breath and began to talk in a slow and deliberate manner, choosing her words carefully. "Kelly, when Jesse, a man who I was deeply in love with, was murdered, you were the one who solved the crime. I know your husband is the sheriff and found out many things related to the crime, but you were the one who put two and two together. As a favor to me, and I know I have no right to ask this, would you please try to find out who killed Dede? She was my best friend. I want to know who killed her and why."

"Sophie, I'm not a professional crime solver. Portland is a big city, and I imagine there will be lots of police and detectives involved in this, all far more knowledgeable about crime than me."

"Please, please. They don't know her. You know me and through me, you met her. You cooked what was probably her last meal. That has to mean something. Please try to see what you can do. I have a feeling you can help, and my feelings are usually right." She began to cry softly and looked at Kelly with a pleading look in her eyes.

Kelly sighed deeply. "Well, if I'm going to stay here and help with the restaurant, it probably would make sense to see if I can find out anything about her death, but only under one condition."

"What is that?"

"You have to promise me you won't breathe a word of this to Mike. He doesn't like me to get involved in murder cases, and he worries about me if I do."

"I understand. You have my word. I won't say a thing to him."

"Good. Now I have a request of you. You're a far better cook than you led me to believe. I want you to be with me in the restaurant. We'll do this together, working as a team. Remember, you told me you often pretended a large number of people would be eating the food you prepared. Well, now they actually will be."

For the first time in the past several hours, Sophie smiled. "I think I would like that, and it would make me feel I was doing something for Donatella. She gave me so much in friendship and introduced me to many of the wonderful people who live in the Pearl District. Yes, I'll do it. Let's get started."

"Give me a couple of minutes. I need to call Roxie and Mike. Why don't you go over to the restaurant and talk to the staff? For now, tell them that Donatella had asked you a long time ago to help in the restaurant if she wasn't able to for some reason. You know the staff, and it will probably be a relief to them to find out that the restaurant isn't going to close. I'll be there as soon as I finish my calls. It will probably be really busy for the next few days. It's been my experience when something bad happens, people need to get together and talk about it. Kelly's Koffee Shop has always been the place where the people go in Cedar Bay when something like this happens, and I imagine the people will come to Mangia! Mangia! for the same reason."

Good grief. What have I done? Heading up one of the finest Italian restaurants on the West Coast and trying to solve a murder at the same time. I should have my head examined, and I'll probably be looking at divorce papers if Mike finds out. My fingers will have to be permanently crossed behind my back from now on whenever I talk to him.

CHAPTER EIGHT

Kelly called Roxie first to ask her if she could manage the coffee shop for a few extra days while Kelly stayed in Portland to help Sophie oversee Mangia! Mangia!

"Thanks, Roxie. I won't be gone longer than a week. Naturally, I'll pay you extra for all of this, and I'm so glad your friend enjoys working there and is such a big help to you. Again, thanks for being so understanding."

One down and now for the hard part.

"Hi, Mike. I wasn't planning on calling you today, but it's been an interesting morning. Actually, I wish you were here. I think your expertise in matters relating to murder would be appreciated." She told him everything that had happened, and that Sophie had asked her to stay for several days and help out at the restaurant.

Mike remained completely quiet while she spoke. When she finished, he said, "Kelly, I can understand why Sophie feels she needs you to help keep the restaurant open and certainly, you're the logical one to help. What I don't like is having you work in a place where the owner was just murdered. For all you know, it could be someone who was jealous of the success of the restaurant, and that person might decide to return to the scene and try to murder you. I don't know how in the devil you do it, but you seem to attract murder like some dogs attract fleas," he said in an exasperated voice.

"Mike, how could I possibly know this was going to happen when I agreed to cater Sophie's party? This is just a random happenstance. Really, I'll be fine. Detective Masters is handling the case, and he seems very competent. It's not like it happened in Cedar Bay. There were so many police and detectives at the house today I couldn't even begin to count them."

"Kelly, would you promise me two things?"

"Sure, Mike, what?" she said mentally crossing her fingers behind her back.

"First of all, I want Rebel with you at all times. Unfortunately, I have several cases here that need my attention. If I can't be there to protect you, at least he can be there to look out for your safety. Secondly, promise me you will not become involved in solving this murder in any way. Do we have an understanding?"

"Yes. I promise you I won't do anything on my own that would cause me to get involved in the case, but as far as Rebel with me at all times, that's going to be hard to do. It's one thing for me to have a dog in my coffee shop in Cedar Bay, but I don't think I can get by with it here in Portland. I'm sure someone would report me. What I will do is have him right outside the back door of the kitchen. When I'm at the restaurant I'll be spending most of my time there, and although I haven't been in it yet, I'm sure there's a back door. There might even be an office, and he could stay there. He'll be with me the rest of the time, and Sophie's home is very safe."

"All right. I can live with that, but I want you to call me every night, and if for any reason, you start to feel threatened or unsafe, promise me you'll leave and come home. By the way, did you take your gun with you?"

"I promise," she fibbed, looking up towards heaven and hoping to make a deal with whatever powers reigned there if and when she ever got there. "And yes, I do have the gun with me, so I'll be fine."

"Good, I'm glad to hear that. That makes me feel a little better. Kelly, I love you. Be safe." She ended the call and told Rebel to come with her. It was time to begin working at Mangia! Mangia!

*****

Kelly opened the door of Mangia! Mangia! and was immediately greeted by Carlotta, the hostess she'd met when she and Sophie had eaten there in what seemed a lifetime ago, but in reality, was only the day before yesterday.

"Welcome Mrs. Reynolds. I understand you're the new chef of Mangia! Mangia! Congratulations, and please let me know if there's anything I can do to make this new job easier for you."

"Thank you, Carlotta. First of all, I'd like to make this change as seamless as possible. I'm sure people will be asking you what's going to happen to the restaurant. Simply tell them a visiting chef will be filling in until a new permanent chef is selected, but that nothing will be changed in the interim. That should make them feel better. Secondly, if there's anything you can tell me that you think I should know, please don't hesitate. This is all pretty new to me. Also, do you know if Mrs. DeLuca had any enemies?"

"Ever since I heard that Mrs. De Luca had been murdered, I've been trying to think why someone would do it. Although almost everyone loved her, there are a few people I'd want to talk to if I were in charge of solving her murder."

"With your work station right here next to the front door, you've probably had a better opportunity than anyone to observe what's going on here at the restaurant."

"Mrs. Reynolds, what I'm going to tell you is just stuff I've heard. I don't have any real facts to back it up, and I'd really appreciate it if you didn't say that anything I'm about to tell you came from me."

"I can certainly promise you that. Rest assured I won't tell anyone I learned anything from you."

Carlotta looked around to see if anyone could overhear what she was about to say. Satisfied, she began, "A couple of people came to my mind. That snooty food critic for the Portland Gazette, Bill Hossam, has eaten here several times in the last month. A friend of mine who knows him told me that Hossam didn't think our food was all that good. He's the only food critic in Portland who hasn't written a review of our restaurant."

"Did Mrs. DeLuca know Mr. Hossam had visited the restaurant?"

Carlotta nervously looked down at her hands and then abashedly looked up at Kelly. "I told her. I thought she should know."

"I think that was the right thing to do. When did you tell her?"

"It was the afternoon of the night you came to dinner. I remember, because she was quite upset. She told me he better not publish a bad review, because it could really hurt her business."

"Do you know if she did anything about it?"

"I'm pretty sure she called him. I needed to tell her to get more salt for the salt shakers on the tables, and I went back to her office. The door to her office was closed, but I could hear her screaming on the telephone, and I realized she was talking to Mr. Hossam. I overheard her tell him that if he wrote a bad review for Mangia! Mangia! she'd personally make sure it was the last review he ever wrote for the Gazette. I don't know what happened after that."

"You know, Carlotta, you look the way my daughter used to look when she wanted to tell me something, but wasn't exactly sure what I would think about it after she told me. Is there something else I should know?"

"Mrs. Reynolds, you didn't hear this from me, but there is a very wealthy woman who lives here in the Pearl District, not far from the restaurant. She brings a lot of people to the restaurant, and a few weeks ago she asked Mrs. DeLuca to cater a dinner party in her home. Mrs. DeLuca didn't like to do catering, because she felt she needed to be at the restaurant, but Elena Wright insisted, and because she is such a good customer, Mrs. DeLuca agreed to it. Miss Wright wanted scallops served to her guests, and I remember Mrs. DeLuca telling me that she really didn't like to fix seafood when she catered, because she worried something might be wrong with the shellfish and the dinner guests might become ill.

"Evidently the dinner party was being held in honor of a friend of Miss Wright's who lived in the Midwest. This particular person had never eaten scallops and had a severe allergic reaction to them during the dinner party. Fortunately there was a doctor at the dinner party, and he treated her immediately. Miss Wright refused to believe her guest had become ill because she'd insisted on serving scallops without inquiring as to whether or not her special guest or anyone else had any food allergies."

"Good grief. That really is dangerous. That poor woman could have gone into anaphylactic shock and died. What happened to her?"

"Miss Wright's guest recovered, but she blamed Mrs. DeLuca for serving bad scallops. It didn't help that all the papers got wind of it and made Miss Wright out to be a bad hostess for not finding out whether or not any of her guests had food allergies. Miss Wright's claim to fame, besides being the only child of a rich lumber baron, is her entertaining. She has a reputation in Portland as being the 'hostess with the mostest,' if you know what I mean. Evidently a number of people have declined her invitations to dinner parties since then, and she blamed Mrs. DeLuca."

"Well, that's interesting. I suppose she might have had a motive for killing Mrs. DeLuca, and Mr. Hossam might have felt she'd threatened him. If I was going to make a list of possible suspects, I think I'd be well advised to include the two of them in the list based on what you've told me. Thanks, Carlotta, I really appreciate your confiding in me, and don't worry. I never heard any of this from you."

Kelly took a deep breath and walked through the dining area to the kitchen which was located towards the rear of the building.

CHAPTER NINE

It was 11:00, only a few hours after the gruesome discovery of Donatella's body, and the restaurant was scheduled to open for lunch at 11:30. Kelly walked into the kitchen and stood for a moment, staring in amazement at what looked like orchestrated chaos taking place before her very eyes. People were cooking, chopping, going in and out of the large walk-in refrigerator, taking things out of the ovens, and putting things in the ovens. Over in a corner Sophie was in a deep conversation with a handsome looking young man. Kelly walked over to them.

Sophie looked up and said, "Kelly, I'd like you to meet Chef Nico Bassi. He was Dede's sous chef. I told him I want him to act as chef, but for the time being, I want all of the dishes to remain as they were when Dede was chef. He agrees with me. We're just going over the menu. He's giving me an overview of how the kitchen works and who is responsible for what. I think we're very lucky to have such a fine staff. I really believe we can pull this off."

A tall muscular blond man with a tattoo of a chef's knife prominent on his right forearm stood up and held out his hand to Kelly. "It's a pleasure to meet you. Mrs. Marchant has told me what a good chef you are and about your restaurant in Cedar Bay. I consider it an honor to have the opportunity to work with you."

"Thank you, but please call me Kelly, and call Mrs. Marchant,

Sophie. We'll be working too close together for formalities. The restaurant opens in a half an hour. What can I do to help other than get out of your way?"

"Kelly, if you could handle anything that happens in the front of the house, I would appreciate it," Nico said. "Some of the staff is a little nervous about everything that's happened today. I'd like to be able to stay here in the kitchen with the kitchen staff until they feel comfortable. They're worried that the restaurant is going to close and they won't have jobs."

"I thought Sophie told you that was not going to happen."

"Actually when she first walked into the kitchen she told me that, but nevertheless, some of the staff think we're going to close after today or when the food runs out."

"Nico," Sophie said, "Let me repeat what I told you earlier. I have money to order the food and take care of the employee expenses, so please tell the staff I will take care of any costs that the restaurant incurs until a final decision is made concerning its continued operation. We don't even know what's in Dede's Will or if she made arrangements in it for the continued operation of the restaurant."

"Sophie," Kelly said, "why don't you stay here with Nico and learn everything you can about what's taking place here in the kitchen? I'm going to talk to the bartenders and the wait staff and assure them that nothing will change for the foreseeable future."

She left the kitchen and walked over to the two bartenders who were standing behind the bar engaged in a deep conversation. She overheard one of them saying, "Well, now that she's dead, her lover's ex-wife probably won't be coming in here anymore. Thank heavens. She's got that redhead temper and drinks way too much. I've had to cut her off several times. Didn't want to be the one sued for letting her drive when she was drunk."

The other one replied, "Yeah, me too. I never understood why Mrs. DeLuca didn't just refuse to serve her."

"You know what a soft touch she was. She felt sorry for Mr. Ramos' ex-wife because he'd left her for Mrs. DeLuca. Guess it was quite the scandal when he divorced her, but she had a lot of moxie to come in here and make the scenes she did. I'll give her credit for one thing though, she was careful to never do it at mealtimes, just in the afternoons. I remember one time she got in Mrs. DeLuca's face and accused her of stealing her husband. That was the only time I saw Mrs. DeLuca completely lose it and really get mad. She told her to leave and never come back. Actually, I think you were off that day. It was only a few days ago."

Kelly cleared her throat, and they both turned to her. "Hi, I'm Kelly Reynolds, I just wanted to introduce myself and assure you that the restaurant is going to remain open. A friend of Mrs. DeLuca's, Sophie Marchant, and I will be running it for the time being. Actually, Sophie was one of Mrs. DeLuca's closest friends and was in here a lot. You probably know her."

"Of course. That makes me feel good. She's good people," the taller of the two men said. "How can we help?"

"I don't know much about serving alcohol. I own a restaurant, well, actually it's a coffee shop, in Cedar Bay, but we don't serve alcohol. Can you give me a quick course in how it works here?"

For the next fifteen minutes the two bartenders instructed her in what they did to keep the bar up and running. They showed her how they gauged the amount of liquor that went into a mixed drink, reviewed the wine list, how to operate the cash register, where they put used glasses, and anything else that came to their minds about the bar business.

"You must take in a lot of money here at the bar. Who picks it up, and where does it go?"

"Mrs. DeLuca picked it up every couple of hours. She did the same with the reception desk, because the servers took their credit card payments or cash to the register there. She has a floor safe in her office, and she put the money in there. Rango Security Company comes every morning to collect the receipts from the day before and then deposits the money in her bank account."

"Thanks, based on that procedure, I'll continue to do the same."

She walked into Donatella's office and pulled back several throw rugs until she found the floor safe. *Swell, I've found the safe, but I have no idea how to open it. I'll have to make some other arrangement for the money until I can find out the combination.*

While she was contemplating what to do next, the phone on Donatella's desk rang. She crossed the small room in several steps and answered it. "This is Kelly Reynolds."

"Mrs. Reynolds, it's Carlotta. I'm sorry to bother you, but there's a man here at the reception desk who says he's Mrs. DeLuca's lawyer, and he needs to talk to you. I told him you and Mrs. Marchant were going to run Mangia! Mangia! for the time being, and he said he'd like to talk to her as well. I've called the kitchen, and she's on her way."

"Please send him back here to the office. Thanks, Carlotta."

A moment later there was a knock on the door. Kelly opened the door, and a large man dressed in a very expensive-looking grey pinstripe suit walked into the room. His thinning white hair was swept back from his forehead and his sharp blue eyes openly assessed her. He put out his hand, "Hello. I'm George Mitchell, Donatella's attorney, or rather I was."

Sophie walked into the room and greeted the man. She turned to Kelly, "I've been to several dinner parties at Donatella's where George was also a guest. It's good to see you again, George, although I would prefer if it was under different circumstances."

"So would I, Sophie, so would I." He set the large briefcase he'd been carrying on the desk. "Ladies, would you please be seated? I need to talk to you." He opened the briefcase and took out what looked like legal papers with a blue backer attached. "Normally when someone is deceased, I would do a reading of their Will with all of the heirs and family members present in my office a day or two after their death, but time is of the essence here because of the restaurant. Francesca is the primary heir of the estate, and as you know, she isn't capable of understanding what's contained in the Will."

"I'm confused, George, I don't see how this affects either one of us."

"Sophie, it will all be clear in a few moments, you see, Donatella DeLuca willed the Mangia! Mangia! restaurant to you. She made some changes to her Will a month ago, and she told me at the time that you were a superb cook. She said you'd always wanted to cook for people, but you were afraid to, so she wanted you to have the chance."

"*Mon Dieu*, I can't believe it. Mangia! Mangia! left to me? She believed in me enough that she left her restaurant to me? *Non*, this is too much. Shouldn't this go to Francesca?"

"I'm sure it would have if things had been different, but obviously Francesca is not capable of handling it. Donatella provided for Francesca in other ways. She left her house to her as well as the proceeds from the sale of her cookbooks along with a stock brokerage account containing investments she'd made in the stock market. That account alone is worth over five million dollars. There is easily enough money and assets available to continue indefinitely with the type of care she has been receiving."

Kelly looked over at Sophie who appeared to be in a state of shock. "I don't know what to say. I never even thought of owning a restaurant."

"Well, if you choose to sell it at some point, that's your decision. I need your signature on a number of forms that will authorize you to buy provisions for the restaurant from various food and alcohol purveyors as well as changing the bank account to reflect that you're authorized to sign checks for the staff, etc." He took a number of papers out of his briefcase and passed them over to Sophie. "Please sign where the red 'x' appears on each page. My secretary has been very busy since Detective Masters called us this morning with the sad news, but I believe all the necessary paperwork is here.

"I'll be filing Donatella's Will with the probate court this afternoon, and at the same time I will ask the court for an emergency order allowing Sophie to continue operating Mangia! Mangia! until ownership of the restaurant is officially transferred at the close of the probate proceedings."

"Excuse me, Mr. Mitchell," Kelly said, "by any chance do you know the combination to the floor safe? I found the safe, but I have no idea how to open it," Kelly said.

"It's probably in this packet of documents. Donatella gave me an envelope three days ago and told me I was to give it to Sophie if anything ever happened to her. I thought it was a rather strange request at the time. Now I wonder if she had a premonition this was going to happen." He handed the envelope to Sophie.

"I would love to stay and talk to both of you. Actually I would love to stay and order something off of the fabulous lunch menu, but I have to be in court this afternoon, and the judge I'm appearing before is very unforgiving if lawyers show up late in his courtroom." He picked up the papers Sophie had signed and said, "If you have any questions, please call me. Here's my business card, and I wish you luck, Sophie. I'm sure Mangia! Mangia! is in very good hands."

CHAPTER TEN

Given the circumstances, Sophie and Kelly's first attempt at serving lunch and running Mangia! Mangia! was a huge success. As Kelly had predicted, the customers wanted to know what was going to happen. Kelly had instructed Carlotta, the bartenders, and the wait staff as to how they should handle the questions, and fortunately for everyone, it went very smoothly. The customers seemed genuinely relieved that the popular restaurant was going to remain open.

Just as the crowd was beginning to thin out, Carlotta motioned Kelly over to the reception desk. "What is it Carlotta?"

"The man sitting at the table by himself two tables back from the windows is the restaurant critic, Bill Hossam. He's the one I told you about. I thought you'd want to know."

"Oh great. Why is he here? Is he on a restaurant death watch? He probably wants to see if we can keep the restaurant open. I'll let Sophie know and see what she says. I don't know if it's proper for me to introduce myself and welcome him or what." She hurried back to the kitchen.

"Sophie, we apparently have our first challenge. I haven't had a chance to tell you, but evidently the restaurant critic from the Portland Gazette was getting ready to write a bad review of Mangia! Mangia!, and Donatella confronted him about it by phone. He's here now. Carlotta just pointed him out to me. What do you want to do? Do you want to go talk to him and welcome him? I really don't know what's customary and usual in a situation like this."

"I'm sorry to ask you to do this, Kelly, but you're so good with people, I'd really appreciate it if you would take care of it. I think the sensible thing to do would be to welcome him. I have a temper, and if he said anything about Dede, I might ruin any chance we have of getting a good review. Actually, Nico and I were going over some terrific ideas he has about changing the menu. I have to say I'm impressed with his ideas, although Dede told me once that only restaurants that weren't successful changed their menus. She told me she was certain that's why Mangia! Mangia! was popular, because people felt comfortable coming to a restaurant they knew would have the same food they liked the last time they were there."

"All right. It's your restaurant, but this is not my favorite thing to do. Wish me luck."

"Excuse me, Kelly," Nico said. "Bill Hossam has a reputation in the industry for being very nasty. You should see some of the scathing reviews he's written about other restaurants. I always feel sorry for the owner whenever he publishes one. He dislikes more restaurants than he likes. I just hope ours isn't going to be one of them."

"Thanks. I'll keep that in mind and not take anything he says personally. Okay," she said, taking a deep breath. "Here probably goes nothing." She walked out of the kitchen and over to his table.

"Hello. I understand you're Bill Hossam from the Portland Gazette. I'm Kelly Reynolds, a good friend of the new owner. Welcome to Mangia! Mangia!"

Looking like a college professor in his sport coat with leather patches at the elbow, a bow tie, and horned rim glasses, the balding middle-aged man looked up from the antipasto platter he had ordered. "New owner? That was fast. Who is it?"

"The new owner was a very good friend of Donatella DeLuca, the former owner and the woman who was found murdered this morning. Her name is Sophie Marchant."

"Never heard of her. What are her credentials for running a restaurant like this? Does she have any formal training? What other restaurants has she owned?"

"I don't believe she has any formal training, but Mrs. DeLuca thought enough of her skills that she provided in her Will that Mangia! Mangia! was to be bequeathed to her. That certainly says a lot about her faith in Mrs. Marchant."

"Not really. Donatella never tried anything new, and this restaurant reflects it. Everything on this menu was probably on a similar menu fifty years ago. I was getting ready to write a review of it when I heard she'd died. I was curious to see if anything would change. From what you're telling me, I guess not. Might as well write my review and get it over with. Between a new owner and my review, I predict a very short life for this restaurant. Be good riddance. Donatella recently threatened me and told me I'd be very sorry if I wrote a bad review. I don't like being threatened. Quite frankly, this place doesn't deserve a good review. I can make or break a restaurant with my reviews, and this one probably needs to be broken," he said arrogantly.

"I'm sorry you feel that way. Actually, I think the new owner is going to be making some changes. Would you do her a favor and hold off reviewing the restaurant for a few days or at least until she has a chance to put some of the new dishes on the menu?"

"Why should I? New dishes from someone who's never owned a restaurant and doesn't have any formal training – it'll probably be some Italian form of a tuna noodle potato chip casserole."

"I don't think so. Donatella had a very good sous chef who was anxious to put some of his creations on the menu. I believe Mrs. Marchant is going to give him the chance."

"That piques my curiosity. Tell this mysterious Mrs. Marchant that I will give her one week. I'll be back then, and if the new dishes don't live up to what you're telling me, I'll publish the review I was planning to prior to the untimely death of Mrs. DeLuca."

"Thank you, Mr. Hossam. I appreciate your courtesy, and I'm sure Mrs. Marchant will too. *Buon appetito*," she said as she walked away from his table, trying to look as if nothing had happened.

Sophie took one look at Kelly when she entered the kitchen and said, "*Chérie*, it was that bad?"

"That is the most repulsive man I think I've ever met. He was hoping the restaurant would fail, and then his review would be justified."

"When is he going to publish it?" Nico asked.

"I don't know. I bought a little time. His main complaint seems to be that the dishes served here are like the dishes that were served in Italian restaurants fifty years ago. He said there was nothing new or innovative on the menu." She turned to Sophie. "I didn't know what else to say, so I told him the new owner and the sous chef were making plans to introduce a fantastic new menu. I asked him if he would hold off publishing his review until he'd had a chance to try the new menu. He said he would come back in a week and try it. I'm sorry, Sophie, that was the best I could do. I was afraid that with Donatella's death and a bad review, it would mean the end of the restaurant."

"Nico, now we don't have a choice. How soon can you have those new dishes of yours ready to be served to the diners?"

"I've tested all of them several times. I'll tell the staff they'll be on the menu tomorrow and instruct them as to what they should say when the diners ask about them. We'll need to get temporary paper menus printed up by tomorrow and if the dishes are well received, get new regular menus printed. I'll make a list of what I'll need."

"Give me the names of the dishes and their descriptions. I'll go down the street to Hank's Print Shop. I've had him print paper menus for me when I've entertained. He's a very interesting individual, but he'll get it done and on time," Sophie said.

"I'll have them to you in half an hour. We'll have the wait staff give the diners a paper menu along with the regular menus. This is going to work. Thanks for believing in me, Sophie," he said, grinning as he wrote out the new menu items as fast as he could.

"Nico. Make it legible. Hank will have to be able to read your writing in order to typeset it."

"Will do," he muttered, totally engrossed in creating his new menu.

"Kelly, let's go to the office," Sophie said. "I want to talk to you while Nico writes out the items to be included in the new menu."

A few minutes later they sat in the restaurant's office, trying to absorb everything that had happened in the last few hours. "Kelly, do you really think I can do this?" Sophie asked.

"Absolutely. I think you're lucky to have Nico. If you can get a good restaurant review, that would be fabulous. You don't have a choice. I know Donatella didn't want to change the menu, but if you don't, you could be looking at the restaurant closing before you even have a chance to see what it can do."

"I just hope I'm not, how do you say it? Something about being in the water and drowning?"

"That's not quite the way the saying goes. I think you're trying to say 'in over your head,' but I'm sure you'll rise to the occasion and not drown. I think we could both use a cup of coffee. Just sit for a minute, and I'll go get us some."

As she walked into the dining room area she saw a red-haired woman sitting at the bar speaking angrily in a loud voice and gesturing in a threatening manner at the tall bartender.

CHAPTER ELEVEN

Kelly walked to the far end of the bar and motioned to the bartender that she wanted to speak with him. He said something to the woman seated at the bar and walked over to where Kelly was standing.

"What's going on?" she asked.

"I just told that woman I wouldn't serve her another martini. She started yelling at me and told me I didn't know who she was. I know who she is, all right. Every bartender at Mangia! Mangia! knows who she is. She generally comes in after the lunch crowd leaves and has a couple of martinis. She gets real mouthy the more she drinks. Her name is Tina Ramos. She's the ex-wife of the man Mrs. DeLuca was seeing before her death. She's as mean as a rattlesnake, and she's got a really bad temper."

"Stay here. I'll go talk to her and ask her to leave. What exactly did you say to her?"

"I told her I couldn't serve her another martini, because I thought she was becoming intoxicated, and I was the one who could be sued."

"Thanks. I imagine this isn't part of your job description."

"You've got that right."

Kelly walked up to the beautiful redhead with brilliant deep blue eyes and a porcelain complexion. She was wearing a pink sheath dress which hugged her well-developed curves. "Mrs. Ramos, I'm Kelly Reynolds, a friend of the new owner of Mangia! Mangia! I'm sorry, but I'm going to have to ask you to leave, and I'd prefer it if you didn't come back."

"What are you talking about?" she slurred. "I'm just doin' a little celebratin'. You know the woman who stole my husband from me's dead. Seems they found her body this mornin'. Serves her right for doin' that to me. Wish it would've happened sooner. Nothin' wrong with me. Tell that idiot bartender to get me another martini."

"No. You've had enough. I don't want to have to call the police and have them arrest you for disturbing the peace. I'm trying to help you. Please leave and don't come back."

"You'd be celebratin' too if the woman who took your husband wound up deader than a doornail. Me and Mitch were happy until she started showin' up like a female dog in heat. Mitch never was able to resist a woman in heat. Shoulda' told her that's the way he is. Wasn't the first time it happened, but he never wanted a divorce before. I always took him back. So who gets the restaurant, Mitch?"

"No. The new owner is a woman by the name of Sophie Marchant, a friend of Donatella's."

"Yeah, sure. Like she could have any friends. Her with her sexy Italian eyes and walk, teasin' every man she saw. Heard Mitch was gonna star her in some TV show called Dining with Donatella. He probably thought her show was gonna save him and his station from bankruptcy. He never paid me any alimony, so I'm not gonna lose anything, but he sure is. Like his television station. Bet she didn't know how broke he was. Whoever put her under the sod actually got both of them. Mitch'll probably have to declare bankruptcy, and Donatella's dead. I like those words. Got a real nice sound to them. Donatella's dead. Kind of rolls off the tongue real nice and easy."

"Mrs. Ramos, if you don't leave now, I'm going to tell the

bartender to call the police. I'm giving you one more chance to leave. Now."

Tina struggled to get down from her perch on the bar stool and almost fell in the process, stumbling when her foot reached the floor. Kelly put a hand on her elbow to steady her. "Don't touch me. I didn't give you permission to touch me. I'm leavin', and I won't be back. I was jes' celebratin' the death of Donatella. You can color me happy. Mitch will get his, and she sure got hers, just like she deserved."

She staggered unsteadily towards the front door and opened it. "Tell yer' friend this probably won't last long. Donatella's dead, and her restaurant will soon be just as dead as she is," she said with a parting salvo. Tina walked out into the afternoon sun and Kelly watched her through the window, weaving along the sidewalk as she attempted to hail a cab.

Thank heavens she has sense enough to get a cab and not try to drive. If the restaurant review doesn't ruin us, a drunken customer in an auto accident might be the final death knell.

"Thanks, Mrs. Reynolds," the bartender said. "I didn't know she was that drunk. I only served her two martinis. She must have been drinking before she came here. I hope that's the last we see of her. I really appreciate you going to bat for me."

"Not a problem. Glad I was able to help. Hate to categorize people, but she sure has the temperament of the classic redhead fireball, and in her case the fire is obviously fueled by alcohol."

Kelly turned and walked back to the kitchen to see how Nico and Sophie were doing.

"*Chérie*, would you do me a favor? Could you take the new menu to Hank's Print Shop for me? His shop is just a few doors down the street. I'd go, but there is so much for me to learn. I think my time would be better spent staying here."

"Of course. I'll take care of it. What kind of paper do you want it printed on and how many copies? Should I ask him if he could send the bill here, or do you want me to pay for it?"

"Tell him I'm the new owner of the restaurant and to send the bill here. He knows I'm good for it. Nico, I think black ink on a pale rust colored paper would work. That's similar to the color of the regular menu. Would that work for you?"

"Yes. That sounds great. Kelly, I think you should order about five hundred copies. We usually wipe down the regular menus each day, but these won't have a protective coating on them, so we'll probably have to throw a lot of them away after we use them."

"Okay. See you later."

CHAPTER TWELVE

When Kelly walked out the back door of the restaurant she involuntarily blinked as the sun on the warm August day was shining brightly. "Rebel, come," she said to the big boxer who was sleeping by the door. They walked between the restaurant and the building next door, turning left onto the sidewalk as they started walking towards Hank's Print Shop.

Well, this is probably going to be my only time to explore the Pearl District and walking halfway down one street is not what I really had in mind. However, given everything that's happened, I don't think there's any way Sophie and I will be able to take the exploratory trip I had in mind.

She stopped and looked in the window of the antique shop that was next to the restaurant. The eclectic art deco style of the store was reflected in the sleek, geometric shapes and angular patterns of the furniture and decorative accessories. Highly lacquered veneer tables, chrome lamps, brightly colored Native American rugs, and exotic influences from Mexico, Africa, Egypt and Asia fit in perfectly with the feel of the Pearl District. It was a shop that cried out to be explored, and Kelly wished she had the time to do just that, but it wasn't meant to be.

Next to it was a postage stamp size dog park. Benches and bright red fire hydrants had been placed in a small grassy area between two buildings. Owners sat on the benches and their dogs frolicked in the fenced park. Kelly approvingly noticed that a hose to fill water dishes for the dogs was located at the rear of the enclosed area. Rebel stopped at the gate and looked up inquiringly at Kelly as if to say, "We could use a little break. It's been a rough day. Let's go in."

"Sorry, boy, not today. We've got things to do."

They passed an art gallery specializing in pen and ink drawings which were tastefully displayed on brightly colored easels and on the walls of the shop. In keeping with the theme of the nearby dog park, the artist had captured dogs in all kinds of activities. The black and white drawings were a great contrast to the vibrant bright colors which dominated the gallery.

The building next to Hank's was the home of a large yoga studio. As Kelly approached she saw several students entering the studio carrying bright yoga mats in greens, blues, and purples and wearing colorful yoga tops and pants. The studio window was filled with a large blow-up photograph of students sitting with their eyes closed and their hands on their knees in the classic serene lotus posture. The photograph made those who passed by the window want to feel as stress-free as the students in the class seemed to be. It was a great advertisement for yoga.

When she got to the print shop she opened the glass door that had the words "Hank's Print Shop" emblazoned in gold letters on it. She stepped into the shop and shook her head in confusion. Fine art covered the walls and a beautiful large blue silk Chinese rug had been placed on the highly polished wooden floor. The bell above the door rang when Kelly opened it and moments later a small man wearing a leather apron over bermuda shorts walked out of the back room.

"May I help you?" the man asked. Kelly smiled in befuddlement at the bearded man who wore diamond stud earrings and had a pony tail held in place by a barrette that looked to be made of onyx. "I'm really confused. The sign on the door says 'Hank's Print Shop,' but I've never been in a print shop like this one."

"Good. That's exactly the response I was looking for when I

opened the shop. I didn't want it to be like all the others, and this being the Pearl District, I figured I could get away with it." He grinned and held out his hand. "I'm Hank Jones, the owner. I don't think we've met."

"No. My name is Kelly Reynolds. A friend of mine, Sophie Marchant, is the new owner of Mangia! Mangia! and I'm helping her."

"I heard about Donatella's murder. That's so sad. She was one of my customers, and I loved to eat at her restaurant. Matter of fact, I never charged her for what I did for the restaurant, and she never charged me for the food I ate. It was a great arrangement. So Sophie's going to take it over. I've known Sophie for some time, and it sort of surprises me. I know she loves to cook, but I didn't know she had any restaurant experience."

"She doesn't. I own a coffee shop in Cedar Bay, and I came up here to cook dinner for a party she was giving for Donatella. When she found out about Donatella's death, she asked if I'd stay for a couple of extra days and help her. The reason I'm here is I need five hundred temporary menus prepared. She told me you've done things like that for her dinner parties."

"Sure. I can do that. When does she need them?"

"Tomorrow. I know it's really short notice, but we're having a bit of an issue with a food critic from the Portland Gazette, and we need to change the menu immediately."

"No problem. Business is a little slow today, so I can get them out before we close. That food critic wouldn't happen to be Bill Hossam, would it?"

"Yes, do you know him?"

"Not personally. I do work for a lot of restaurants in the district. He's given a couple of them reviews that were so bad they had to close. I'd sure hate to see that happen to Sophie's restaurant."

"I met him earlier today, and he seems like a really mean-spirited man. He said he thought the food at Mangia! Mangia! was like, I guess the kids of today would say, so yesterday. Sophie and I decided there was no choice but to offer some new dishes that Nico, the sous chef, has wanted to try."

"I hope it works. I really like Sophie, and I'd like to see her make a go of it. I'll get right on these and drop them by when I close this evening. Tell Sophie I'd like to continue the working arrangement I had with Donatella. I'll do the work for her, eat at the restaurant occasionally, and we'll call it even."

Kelly laughed. "I'm sure that will be fine with her. Here's the new menu. She wants it in black ink on pale rust colored paper."

"No problem. Well, better get to work on these. Nice meeting you."

"Thanks, and you really have created a special shop. I'm sure everyone who comes here tells you that."

"Yeah, pretty much," he said as he walked into the back room, "but that's exactly what I want them to say. Hey, it's the Pearl District, and all of us who live and work here are free spirits."

CHAPTER THIRTEEN

Kelly spent the rest of the remaining afternoon meeting with Nico and Sophie as the three of them prepared to launch the new menu the following day. Nico gave her a list of the foods he wanted for the dishes and which food purveyors she should call to obtain some of the rarer ingredients. All of them promised to have the needed foods at the restaurant by 9:00 the next morning.

"Kelly, Sophie, I think this is really going to work. I want to push two entrees - a seafood bucatini and a lasagna. Both are pasta recipes I learned from my grandmother. They're quite different from the usual recipes for those dishes, and I'm sure the diners will love them. They're a classy take on timeless comfort food dishes. The bucatini has several kinds of seafood in a marinara sauce which has been enhanced by some spices. I let the sauce cook for a long time so the flavors can marry. Sometimes I use lobster in the dish, but I think we'll begin with shrimp, mussels, and some clams.

"By the way Kelly, Sophie told me about a frozen key lime pie you made last night that she said was fabulous. I looked at your recipe and took the liberty of adding some silvered almonds to the topping to give it an Italian feel. It will be a nice addition to the heavier desserts that are on the menu. Those are the three main new things we'll be offering. I've updated some of the pasta and vegetable dishes, but I'm really hoping to make those three dishes the new signature dishes of Mangia! Mangia! Sound good?"

"Yes," Sophie said. "Nico, I've never done anything like this, so I have to trust your restaurant judgment. I not only hope it works because I want to keep the restaurant open, but I also want to do Dede proud. She entrusted me with what she valued most other than her daughter, and I feel an obligation to live up to her faith in me. Do you both understand what I'm trying to say?"

"Absolutely," Kelly said, "and I'm sure Nico feels the same way. You can rest assured we both will do everything we can to make this work for you."

The evening dinner crowd started to arrive shortly after 7:00. Some were returning customers, while others were new and wanted to eat at Mangia! Mangia! before it closed, or so the rumor mill was predicting. Waiters were busy carrying food to hungry guests while in the kitchen pulsating background music matched the orchestrated cadence of the cooks' movements as they began their kitchen dance, a dance that required many steps so all of the components of the meal were ready at the same time.

"Mrs. Reynolds, Carlotta would like to see you out front," one of the waiters said as he came into the kitchen and grabbed a plated meal.

"Wonder what's up now? I'm not sure I can handle another crisis," Kelly said to Nico and Sophie. "I'll be back shortly."

"What is it, Carlotta?" she asked the receptionist a few minutes later.

"Kelly, do you remember me telling you about the woman named Elena Wright? She was the one who gave the dinner party where Mrs. De Luca served the scallops, and her guest became very ill."

"Yes. Why do you ask?"

"Well, it's pretty strange. She hasn't come to the restaurant since that incident happened, but she's here tonight. I thought you ought to know."

"Thanks. Which table is she at?"

"Table number 27. It's in the center of the restaurant. There are two women seated at the table. She's the one wearing the red hat with the purple scarf thrown over her shoulder."

Kelly introduced herself to diners at several of the tables near Elena's, and when she reached her table she said, "Hello and welcome to Mangia! Mangia! My name is Kelly Reynolds. I'm helping the new owner and want to meet as many of the guests as I can. And you are?"

The woman in the red hat looked up at Kelly and said, "Surely you know who I am. I'm Elena Wright. I thought everyone in Portland probably knew me by now, although most of them know me because of what Donatella did to me. You must be new to the area."

"That I am," Kelly said, forcing a smile on her face. "I came up from Cedar Bay to help a friend of mine. Is this your first time at the restaurant?"

"It's the first time I've been here in several weeks. I used to be a very good customer, but that was before Donatella tried to poison a guest of mine with bad scallops she served at a dinner party I was hosting. She never admitted her mistake and tried to put the blame on me, telling everyone I should have asked my guest if she had any food allergies. It's a good thing there was a doctor at my dinner party, or my guest might have died. The only reason I'm here is to celebrate the closing of this restaurant and a very bad time in my life," she said bitterly. "I'm not surprised Donatella was murdered. I just wish she'd been murdered before she catered my dinner party. She was an evil conniving woman, and I truly hated her for what she did to me."

"Elena, that's enough," her dining partner said in a low but commanding tone of voice.

"Yes, well it's been nice meeting you Mrs. Reynolds. I rather doubt we'll be seeing each other again."

"*Buon appetito,*" Kelly said as she continued on to the next table and introduced herself. When she came to the end of the row of tables she walked over to the reception desk. "Carlotta, do you know the woman who's with Elena?"

"Yes. She's Elena's attorney. They used to come here a lot before the scallop incident. Why?"

"She told Elena more or less to shut up. I was wondering why."

"I don't know. We're sure getting a lot of people in here who Mrs. DeLuca had some kind of trouble with. I just received a call from Chef Pierre DuBois for a reservation for six people at 8:00 tonight. I know he and Mrs. DeLuca weren't friends. This is all very strange."

"I agree. I imagine the people who didn't like her are hoping that the restaurant fails. Would you let me know when Chef DuBois arrives? I'd like to meet him."

"Of course. I'll call the kitchen and let you know."

CHAPTER FOURTEEN

"Kelly, Carlotta said to tell you that Chef DuBois and his party have arrived. They're being served their cocktails right now," Nico said, hanging up the house phone.

"Well, what am I now? Three down and one to go. Let's see. There's Elena Wright, Bill Hossam, Tina Ramos, and who knows, maybe Chef DuBois. All of whom for one reason or another didn't like Donatella and actually seem to be glad that she's dead. For a woman who was supposed to be so popular, it seems that Donatella had quite a few people who weren't all that happy with her. Hopefully, this will be short and sweet." In her mind, Nico was still a suspect, but she certainly didn't want to tell him that. She walked out of the kitchen and into the crowded restaurant dining area.

I wonder if it's always this busy on weeknights. They're standing three deep at the bar, every table in the restaurant is taken, and the reception area is filled with people waiting for tables. And they haven't even tried the new menu which debuts tomorrow at lunch. This bodes well for Sophie and Nico. Hope it continues.

It was impossible to miss Chef DuBois and his party. The table was surrounded by people greeting him. As she got closer to it, she overheard a conversation at a nearby table. "I understand he's going to replace Donatella DeLuca. The television station is going to change the name of the show from Dining with Donatella to Dining with DuBois. They'll probably just delete the name Donatella on the promotional material and insert DuBois. They can even keep the D. Makes it real easy," the man said, laughing.

Could he be right? The station, Mitch's station, is going to hire Chef DuBois to replace Donatella? And so fast? Oh no. It looks like the person who said that might be right. That's Mitch Ramos from the television station sitting at the table with the chef.

"Hello, Mitch. It's nice to see you again," Kelly said. He looked up, clearly shocked to see her. Mitch stood up from his chair and shook her hand. "It's been a very emotional day for me. When Chef Dubois asked me to join him for dinner, I thought it might take my mind off of everything that's happened today," he said in a voice tinged with sadness.

I'll bet. Sure didn't seem to stop you from filling that vacancy for the cooking show. Bet Donatella wouldn't have been too happy about that decision.

"Pierre," he said, turning to the chef as the people he had been talking to returned to their table, "I'd like to introduce you to Kelly Reynolds. She's the woman who catered the dinner for Donatella last night."

The fat pock-marked florid-faced chef with the scraggly goatee took Kelly's hand in his and brought it to his lips. "In my country this is how we greet a beautiful woman. It's a pleasure to meet you," he said insincerely. He turned to the other four people at the table, "Gentlemen, I'd like you to meet Kelly Reynolds." They stood and shook her hand.

"I don't want to keep you from your dinners, but I wanted to welcome you to Mangia! Mangia! I'm sure Mitch has eaten here many times, but if the rest of you haven't, you're in for a treat. And it will be even more of a treat when we change to our new and exciting menu tomorrow."

"Why is the menu being changed?" Mitch asked. "I know Donatella wanted it to stay as it always has been."

"The new owner, Sophie Marchant, and her sous chef, felt it was a bit out of touch with what people want in a modern Italian restaurant. I think you'll be pleasantly surprised."

"Well, no matter what you do to this tired and dated restaurant, I'm sure it won't affect the popularity of my restaurant, Le Toque. As a matter of fact, after my show airs next week, I definitely will be the owner of the most popular restaurant in the Pearl District, if not all of Portland, and who knows, maybe even the West Coast," Chef DuBois said in a pompous and arrogant manner. "Donatella was behind the times when it came to her cooking. It was too bad about her being murdered, but I'm glad Mitch called me as soon as he found out and offered me the opportunity to host the show."

Mitch called him immediately after he found out that Donatella had been murdered? So much for grieving over the loss of your steady girlfriend who was about to become the star of your new TV show. Maybe his ex-wife was right. Maybe Donatella was only a way for him to hold onto his failing television station, and now that she's gone, he's hoping that Chef DuBois will be his new ticket to success. I don't think I like this man. No, Mitch, I don't think I'm liking you at all. Something about you just isn't right.

"Mrs. Reynolds, I hope you won't think I'm being rude, but my lawyer and my financial adviser need to talk to Mitch and work out the details of my new television show. I hope you'll watch it. I promise you it will be the best cooking show on the air. People love me and my food," the obnoxious chef said.

"It's been a pleasure to meet you. I look forward to seeing your show and Mitch, it was nice to see you again," Kelly said as she struggled to keep from sounding sarcastic. Willing herself to smile and appear happy, she walked back to the kitchen.

I better tell Sophie about the TV show before she hears it from someone else. With her quick temper, I also better be prepared to keep her from going out to Mitch and Chef DuBois' table and telling them what she thinks of them once she hears the news.

"Sophie, can you come into the office for a moment? I need to talk to you."

A few minutes later Kelly and Sophie were sitting in the office while Kelly took several slow and deliberate sips of water from the glass on the desk. She reached down and petted Rebel, who had decided the carpeted office floor was much more inviting than the concrete slab by the back door. After pausing for a few more moments she related her recent conversation with Mitch and Chef DuBois. Sophie's reaction was exactly what she predicted - instantaneous and explosive with anger. Her hands flew to her heart and her eyes narrowed as she said in a voice filled with anger, "*Mon Dieu!* How dare Mitch besmirch Donatella's name by hiring that sleazy chef. I don't think he's even French. I've noticed his accent is completely wrong when he pronounces certain words."

"Look Sophie, there's nothing we can do except hope his show is a big flop, but from what Mitch's ex-wife told me this afternoon, Mitch needs the show to be a big success, or he might have to declare bankruptcy and lose the television station. Did Donatella ever mention that to you?"

"No, but she was a very private woman. What are you thinking?"

"I'm thinking that maybe Mitch's attentiveness to Donatella was based less on his attraction to her and more on his need to save his television station. Maybe he saw her as the way to do it."

"*Non.* That can't be. If it's true, I'm certain that Donatella didn't know that's how he felt. She was a very high-minded woman, and if she even suspected the only reason for Mitch's attentiveness was because he needed her to help him financially, she wouldn't have allowed their relationship to continue. She really didn't need to do it for the money. I think George Mitchell made that perfectly clear today. Remember, he told us she had numerous assets. No, I'm sure she never suspected that he possibly didn't really love her."

"I need to put the receipts from the bar and the reception desk in the floor safe. Thankfully, we only have a couple more hours, and we can go to your house and get some rest. I honestly don't remember ever being this tired."

"Nico and I have a few more things to discuss about tomorrow. I also need to make some notes on things I need to do tomorrow like alert the newspapers about the change in ownership, and then I'll be ready to go home. Carlotta and Nico can probably handle anything that comes up, and they're used to locking up." She looked at her watch. "Let's plan on leaving in half an hour."

"Fine. I'll meet you in the office." As she made her way towards the front of the restaurant to collect the day's receipts, she had a sinking feeling in her stomach knowing she would have to call Mike as soon as she and Sophie returned to her home.

Today has been a day of putting out one fire after another and the biggest fire of all is yet to come. I promised Mike I wouldn't get involved in trying to solve Donatella's murder, but I don't think I have a choice. I've already discovered a number of people who have motives for killing her, and I'd like to run them by him. After all, he's a sheriff and knows a lot more about solving crimes than I do. Mike isn't going to like it, but he'll probably understand. At least I sure hope so, and if he doesn't, then I'll just have to cross my fingers behind my back and tell him a little white lie.

CHAPTER FIFTEEN

"Sophie, I hope you'll excuse me, but I really am exhausted, and I need to call Mike and tell him what I've learned about some of the possible suspects in Donatella's murder. I value his judgment, even though I don't think he's going to very happy about my getting involved trying to catch the killer."

"Why would he be upset? You solved Jesse's murder, and from what Jesse told me, several others as well. He must be used to you getting involved by now."

"It sounds good on paper, but it doesn't quite work out that way. You see, when I told him I was staying an extra day or two with you, I promised him I wouldn't get involved in the murder investigation. He worries about my safety. As a matter of fact he makes me keep a gun in my purse and wants Rebel to be with me at all times. That's why I took Rebel to the restaurant. I noticed you were a little surprised when I put him by the back door initially and then when I brought him into the office, but I promised Mike that Rebel would be with me. I suppose I can't put off calling him any longer, and if I wait much longer he'll be asleep. See you in the morning. Come on Rebel, time for bed."

Kelly sat down at the desk in the sitting room and called Mike. She knew it would be much easier if she could just get his voicemail, but this was one time she needed to talk to him and looked forward to any advice he could give her.

"Hey, lady, how are you? Before you answer, I want to tell you first how much Lady and I miss you. I really don't want to do this again. Secondly, you know that five extra pounds I'm always fighting? Well, with the caramel sauce I think it's now ten pounds."

"Oh, Mike, I miss you just as much, and I wish you were here. Don't worry about the caramel pounds. I'm sure it looks good on you."

"Wish I thought so. Tell me how it went at the restaurant."

"It's a new learning curve for me. Actually, it went well. Mike, there's something else I need to talk to you about, but before I begin, will you promise me you'll withhold judgment and trust me when I tell you that I didn't do anything deliberately to get involved in the investigations of Donatella's death?"

Mike was quiet for a moment. "Kelly, I have a feeling I am definitely not going to like what you're about to tell me. Just answer one question for me. Are you safe? Actually, I'll make it three questions. That was the first one. The second one is I want to know if your gun is with you, and thirdly, is Rebel with you?"

"The answer is yes to all three questions. Mike, you have to believe me when I tell you what happened at the restaurant today was not something I ever expected would occur. I think what I learned may be very important in solving the case and catching Donatella's killer. I met five people today, and believe it or not, all of them may have had a reason to murder Donatella."

"I'm sorry. It's been a long day, and I admit that I'm a little slow on the uptake tonight. I thought you said you met five people today, all who might have had a reason to murder Donatella. You'll have to excuse me for finding it hard to believe that all five of these people just happened to come to the restaurant and you just happened to find out that they had a motive to kill Donatella? Am I missing something here? Why in the devil do these things happen to you,

Kelly? Have you become some type of a murder solving magnet?"

She sighed. "Mike, I know it's hard to believe, but I really need to hear what you think about what happened today. Could you please just listen to me?"

"Sure, and could you please come home now? Oh, never mind, knowing you, that's not going to happen. Okay, sweetheart, what have you gotten yourself involved in this time?"

"I'm not sure I like the tone of your voice."

"I'm not sure I like you being there," he countered.

She told him everything that had happened during the day and the evening, concluding with Rebel being by her side at the moment and the gun conveniently sitting on the desk in front of her.

"Well, Mrs. Reynolds, I would say you've had a very busy day. What do you need from me? Sounds like you're doing just fine on your own," he said sarcastically.

"Mike, please don't be that way. I really want to hear what you think about all of this."

"Kelly, do you have any idea how much I worry about you? Do you have any idea what I'll be thinking about when I try and get some sleep tonight, if I even get any sleep at all?"

"I'm sorry. Honest, I'm not in any danger. Could I help it if all these things just kind of happened when these various different people showed up at the restaurant?"

"I won't even go there," he said, taking a deep breath. "All right. I know you well enough to know that you're going to get involved anyway, and in my mind, you already are. Let's take these people one by one."

"Mike, could you give me some guidelines on what I should do?"

"My advice is to get in touch with that detective you met at the crime scene, and tell him what you know and come back home. What's his name?"

"Detective Masters."

"Well, switching our conversation to your list of possible suspects, didn't you mention the other night you overheard Donatella and her sous chef having an argument about changing the menu? The first thing that comes to my mind is that it's very convenient that she's gone, and now he gets to change the menu with Sophie's blessing. What's your gut feeling about him?"

"I like him. Yes, Donatella's death did provide him with a way to change the menu, but I can't believe someone would commit murder just so their dishes would be on the menu."

"Trust me, sweetheart, stranger things have happened."

"Well, the only reason the changes are going to be made is because the food critic threatened to write a bad review if they weren't. And don't forget, Carlotta overheard Donatella threatening to ruin the critic if he gave her restaurant a bad review."

"Now tell me what you thought about the food critic."

"He was insufferable. You know, kind of one of those nerdy types who are academics and no one ever liked them until they found some new atom or planet and suddenly everyone thinks they're great. That was kind of the impression I had of him. A nerd who has somehow made it as a food critic."

"If Donatella claimed she could ruin his reputation as a food critic and that was his only claim to fame, that might provide a motive, but how do you think she would be able to do that? Sounds like an empty and perhaps desperate thing for her to say unless Donatella had some information about him that would somehow harm him. Almost sounds like a scenario for blackmail."

"I'm having a hard time thinking of him as a suspect, but theoretically, yes."

"That's two down. What about Mitch's ex-wife?"

"That would be Tina Ramos. She obviously hated Donatella for breaking up her marriage, although from what she said it wasn't the first time that Mitch had been looking in other places for a little affection. According to the bartenders, she's got a really bad temper, so it's possible in a fit of anger she could commit murder. She had a motive, and if she was drunk, she's a definite possibility."

"You didn't care for her, did you?"

"No, but what I saw of her certainly had to be her worst side. Maybe she's a wonderful person when she's not drunk, however, from what the bartender told me, that wasn't the first time they've had problems with her."

"I'd keep her pretty high on the list. And the next one, this Elena Wright?"

"She's kind of like Bill Hossam, the food critic. Her sense of self-importance is wrapped up in what other people think about her. Evidently the incident with Donatella's scallops caused her reputation as one of the leading party givers in the Pearl District to suffer a severe blow. I find it hard to think someone would kill over that, but if her reputation as the 'hostess with the mostest' was all she had, maybe."

"You said her father was a lumber baron. I wonder if I can find out anything about him. I'll look up the name Wright and see what I can come up with."

"Mike, I knew I could count on you. Thank you so much for helping Sophie and me."

"I still think it should be Detective Masters who's helping you and vice-versa. This is way out of my jurisdiction."

"Mike, one thing Sophie mentioned about Chef DuBois was that the accent he placed on some of the French words he used was incorrect. She wonders if he really is French. I did not like that smarmy man. It literally made my skin crawl when he kissed my hand. It was disgusting. I wonder if he could be a complete fake."

"May have disgusted you, but that doesn't mean he's a murderer."

"I know, but the whole television thing smells. First of all he tries to get a show, but Mitch gives the show to Donatella. Then I find out Mitch's television station is in financial trouble, and he calls the chef the morning the woman he loved was murdered and offers the television show to him? Doesn't sound like a very honorable man to me. I don't like the whole television thing, and I don't like either man."

"Lady, I think you've done enough for today. Turn off that wonderfully inquisitive brain of yours and get some sleep. Tomorrow may be another zoo at the restaurant and you also have the new menu to deal with. I'll be curious to see how that goes. I have a little time free in the morning, so I can do some research before I have to attend some meetings I have scheduled. Here's what I'll do. I'll run a check on all these people. I've written their names down while you were talking. Maybe there's something in one of their backgrounds that will give us some type of insight into whether or not they could be the murderer."

"Give us some type of insight, us?" she asked.

"Just a phrase, Kelly. Just a phrase. I'll call you when I know something. And Kelly, this is from Lady, keep the gun on you at all times and Rebel with you. Hear me? Deal?"

"Yes, sir, Sheriff Mike, I promise I will. Deal."

"Kelly, we both know your promises leave something to be desired. How about if you don't keep the promise, you will do all of the dishes, housework, and whatever else I may have in mind," he said laughing.

"I don't know whether I should look forward to that or fear it," she answered.

"Take your pick. Goodnight, sweetheart."

"Goodnight. I love you."

CHAPTER SIXTEEN

When Kelly, Sophie, and Rebel arrived at the restaurant at 10:00 the next morning it was a scene of utter chaos. Nico was trying to get everything ready for the new menu which was to be introduced at lunch. The requested food had been delivered and boxes were stacked on the floor just inside the back door. The kitchen staff was frantically trying put everything away in its proper place before the first diners arrived.

"Nico, did you see the Portland Gazette this morning?" Sophie asked as she began to chop the mound of fresh mushrooms he put in front of her. Kelly watched, impressed by knife skills she didn't know Sophie possessed.

"No, I barely slept trying to wrap my mind around everything that needed to be done today."

"Well, there was a long eulogy to Donatella and at the end the article mentioned that Mangia! Mangia! was under new ownership and a new menu would be debuted at lunch today. I wonder how they found out. Neither Kelly nor I called them."

"That's all we need, a big crowd of hungry diners all ordering the same thing. I'd like to have some time to experiment with the new dishes and try to get them tweaked to perfection. It will be hard to do if everyone is ordering the same dish. I ordered more food than I thought we'd need, but if what you're telling me is true, this could be a disaster. I don't usually let much get to me, but I have to admit I'm a nervous wreck about how these new dishes are going to be received by our customers. If they don't like them, it will not only mean the death of the restaurant, it will be the death of my professional career."

Kelly walked over to him and put her hand on his arm. "Nico, I watched you work all day yesterday, and you're an excellent chef. I know a little about food, and your new menu items are some of the most inventive creations I've ever seen. Just wait. By tonight you'll be the toast of the Pearl District."

He grimaced and looked at her. "Easy for you to say. You'll be going back to your restaurant in Cedar Bay."

"That I will, but I'll be checking in with Sophie. I can't walk away from here and not know what's going to happen. What can I do to help?"

"You can dice these green onions," he said, putting a huge pile on the chopping block. With that Kelly rolled up her sleeves, put on an apron, and started chopping.

At 11:15, Carlotta called the kitchen and Nico took the call. Kelly and Sophie saw him visibly pale while he listened to her. "Thanks, I hope so," he said as he hung up. He turned towards them. "A line of diners has formed in front of the restaurant. She said most of them want to try the new dishes." He yelled to the kitchen staff. "Make more pies, start boiling the noodles, get to your stations. The battle is about to start, and we need to be ready for the onslaught."

Kelly took off her apron. "If it's going to be that busy, I better go out front and help Carlotta."

The restaurant doors opened promptly at 11:30, and no one working at the restaurant even had time to stop for a sip of water until it finally slowed down around 1:30. Kelly walked into the kitchen holding several sheets of notepaper. "Nico, can you take a break for a moment? I want to read a few things to you," she said grinning.

"I decided I'd ask several of the diners who ordered the new dishes if they would mind writing a comment about their meal. Here are a few samples of what they said." She began to read, "I've never eaten anything like this. It was absolutely wonderful and delicious. The seafood bucatini was without a doubt the best thing I've ever had. I wasn't planning on it, but I've decided to come back tonight for dinner, and although I'd like to order the lasagna, I don't think I can get past the perfect combination of seafood, herbs, and spices served over the bucatini. Done this way, it's just like my mother used to make pasta. My taste buds are screaming, 'Have it again.' Here's one for the lasagna. Chef Nico's lasagna has set a new benchmark for the popular dish. Rich in cheese, noodles, and a meaty sauce, there's a perfect blending of spices and rich marinara sauce. My stomach is very, very happy. It is simply the best I've ever had.'"

Nico was standing stone still, a shocked look on his face. Then a smile slowly started to appear at the corners of his mouth and quickly spread into a broad grin across his entire face. "Does this mean we did it?"

"No, it means you did it. Here's one for the frozen key lime pie. The customer wrote that combining the ingredients in the traditional South Florida key lime pie with slivered almonds to give the dish a quasi-Italian feel was sheer genius and resulted in the perfect way to end an Italian meal. Those are just a couple of the numerous favorable comments you received. Congratulations, Nico."

He leaned heavily against the kitchen's central stainless steel counter. "All my life I've lived to hear words like that about my cooking. This is a dream come true. I wish Nonna was alive. She'd be so proud that her cooking was making her grandson famous."

Sophie was quickly beginning to fit into her new role as the owner of Mangia! Mangia! "Okay gang, let's get back to work. If we were that busy for lunch, and no one knew what was going to be on the new menu, I can't begin to imagine what dinner will be like."

A short time later the house phone rang, and Kelly answered it. "Yes, Carlotta, I'll return the calls from the office. Please write down the phone numbers and bring them to me." She turned to Nico and Sophie, "The word's out. Two newspapers have called about the new menu, and one of the television stations wants to interview Nico. I'll talk to them and set it up. What's a good time for you, Nico?"

"Tomorrow morning. I'd be too tired when we finish tonight, and there's too much to do right now. Wow, I can't believe this."

CHAPTER SEVENTEEN

Later that afternoon Kelly talked to the newspapers and the television station and made an appointment for them to interview Nico at ten the next morning. She'd barely hung up the phone when it rang. "Yes, Carlotta." She listened for a moment and then said, "Tell her I'll be out in a few minutes."

She dialed the kitchen. "Nico, this is Kelly. May I speak to Sophie?"

"What's going on?" Sophie asked.

"Something I never thought would happen. Tina Ramos is here and wants to talk to me. Carlotta told me she's waiting for me in the reception area, not the bar, and she doesn't look like she's been drinking. Do you know anything about this?"

"Not a thing, but it's very interesting. I'll be curious to hear what she has to say."

"Me too. I'll let you know when I finish talking to her."

She walked out to the reception area and saw Tina sitting in one of the large red leather chairs, waiting for her.

"Good afternoon, Tina. What can I do for you?"

"If you have a few minutes, I'd like to talk to you."

"Certainly, Carlotta, is it okay if we take the table over by the windows? Would you like a cup of coffee or iced tea, Tina? I'm having some iced tea."

"Please, I'll take the same."

"Carlotta, would you order a glass of iced tea for each of us? Thanks."

They sat down at the table, and Kelly paused for a moment to look at Tina. She looked like a completely different person from the woman Kelly had spoken with yesterday. Kelly thought she was attractive yesterday, but today she was stunning, her red hair a perfect contrast to the deep blue silk pantsuit she wore that accented her eyes.

After the waiter set their iced teas down in front of each of them, Tina began to speak. "I'd like to apologize to you for my behavior yesterday. I know it's not the first time I've had too much to drink here, and I want to assure you it won't ever happen again. I've made a promise to myself that I will never touch alcohol again. Obviously, I'm not a person who handles it well, and that's not who I am at heart. The last couple of months have been very difficult for me. It seems everywhere I turned there was a picture of Mitch and Donatella, and everyone knew he'd left me for her. Frankly, my self-confidence was totally shattered."

"Yes. I can imagine how difficult that might be."

"Thanks. The thing is, I've finally admitted to myself that it really wasn't Donatella's fault. Mitch cheated on me the whole time we were married. My parents left me a large inheritance and looking back, I think that may have been the reason he married me. I believe he left me for Donatella, because he thought she had more money than me, and he may have been right. Anyway, what I told you yesterday about him being in financial trouble was true. He desperately needs a hit show or two to get back the ratings and the advertising dollars his station needs to survive."

"I don't quite know how something like that works. Would you mind explaining it to me?"

"It's all about the big bucks advertising dollars can bring into a station. That's how the stations make their money. When a show's a hit, all the advertisers want to run ads on it, and the more popular the show is, the more the ads cost. I'm sure you've heard about super bowl ads, how popular they are, and how much they cost. Well, it's kind of like that. If you have a hit food show, all the big names in the food industry want to advertise on it, and then if you can get another hit, it keeps growing. I think that was what Mitch was banking on. But there's something else I just learned within the last hour that I think you should know about."

"What's that?"

"Mitch's secretary and I became very good friends over the years. Even when Mitch and I got divorced, it didn't change my relationship with Eva. We're still very close."

"That's not unusual."

"No, I suppose not. She called me a little while ago, and that's really why I'm here. I want to warn you to be careful."

"Me? Careful? What are you talking about?"

"According to Eva, Mitch called Chef Pierre DuBois almost immediately after he found out Donatella had been murdered and offered him the cooking show."

"Yes, I heard that last night. Chef DuBois and Mitch ate a celebration dinner here along with the chef's attorney and three other men."

"Well, from what Eva told me, it may have been a premature celebration. Mitch heard about the new chef here, Nico, and that he had developed several new dishes that were going to be offered today. Eva said Mitch decided to hold off signing the papers hiring Chef DuBois until he saw what was going to happen here at Mangia! Mangia! In other words, he wanted to see if he'd made the right choice in hiring Chef DuBois. Eva said he was thinking that if your new menu was a huge success, it might be a better business decision for him to hire Nico."

"What? I thought it was a done deal, and even if it's not, I still don't see how it affects me other than the restaurant is now owned by a friend of mine, and I'm helping her."

"Kelly, and I hope you don't mind if I call you Kelly, think about it. Everyone knows Chef DuBois has a temper and that he wanted the cooking show, very, very badly. If the show is offered to Nico instead, not only is he going to hate Nico, he'll probably blame you and the new owner for allowing Nico to put his new dishes on the menu and making him into an instant star. In other words, the success of Mangia! Mangia! may be putting you and your friend in jeopardy."

"I can't believe what you're telling me. New dishes are put on restaurant menus all the time, and no one threatens anyone over them."

"It's a little different here in the district. Mangia! Mangia! and Le Toque have been rivals for years, even though one specializes in Italian food, and the other specializes in French food. Add the television show into the mix along with the ego of Chef DuBois, and it makes for a situation that could possibly become explosive and dangerous."

"That simply amazes me. I know I live in a small town, but I can't imagine someone would try to harm us over a television show."

"Human nature is always interesting and none more so than a thwarted chef with a huge ego."

"Tina, thanks for coming here and telling me about this. I'm sure returning to the restaurant after the way you left yesterday was very difficult for you to do, and I want you to know how much I appreciate it. Would you do me a favor? If you hear anything else, please give me a call. I really don't like to think that any one of the three of us could be in danger, but if you feel we need to be warned, please don't hesitate."

"I'd be happy to, and thanks for taking the time to talk to me. I imagine seeing me again wasn't real high on your list of things you wanted to do. If you'll excuse me, I want to go over and apologize to the bartender. Actually, a few apologies over there are probably long overdue." She stood up and walked over to the bar.

If what she says is true, I suppose we could be in danger, even though it still doesn't make a lot of sense to me. I wonder if Mike found out anything about the five people on the list of possible suspects. I probably should give him a call, but first I need to visit Hank and order the permanent menus.

CHAPTER EIGHTEEN

After Tina left, Kelly collected the receipts from the bar and the reception desk and went back to the office to put them in the floor safe she'd found the day before. She knelt down and twirled the dial. Nothing happened. She tried again with no luck.

Darn. I must have reversed a couple of numbers. Better get that combination from the envelope the lawyer left with Sophie and double check the numbers I'm using.

She walked over to the desk and sat down, took a key from the key ring, and unlocked the center drawer where she and Sophie had put the envelope for safekeeping the day before. She took out the slip of paper with the combination written on it and studied it for a moment, realizing she had reversed the numbers.

I probably should check and see what else is in the envelope. Maybe Donatella put something in it that will help me identify the murderer.

She took the contents out of the envelope and looked at them. The one that caught her attention was a handwritten note that read, "If anything should happen to me, please contact Dirk Lewis, a private investigator I hired to investigate Bill Hossam and Chef DuBois. After I read his report I returned it to him, and he can show it to you. His card is attached."

Well that's interesting. I probably better call him and see if I can find out what was in the report. We wondered if she had a premonition that something might happen to her, and I think this confirms it. Good grief. This guy must be something from the looks of his business card. It's not very professional looking. I can't believe someone would put this on a business card, "Dirk The Jerk. The One With The Gun." Just what I need - one more character to add to the mix.

She picked up the phone and dialed the number that was on the business card. The phone was answered immediately by a man who said, "This is Dirk the Jerk. Ain't no job too big or too small. What can I do fer ya?"

Kelly sat back in her chair and looked at the phone. *Donatella hired this guy? I wonder why?* "My name is Kelly Reynolds. I'm a friend of the new owner of Mangia! Mangia! restaurant. The former owner, who I believe was a client of yours, Donatella DeLuca, gave an envelope to her attorney with your business card in it and instructions to call you if anything happened to her. Unfortunately Donatella was murdered yesterday. Her attorney gave the envelope to my friend and me. I just discovered your business card attached to Donatella's note."

"Yeah, I've been wonderin' how long it was gonna be before someone called me. Don't take a whole lot of smarts to figure out that one of them guys I investigated probably offed her."

"I really don't know what you're talking about. Could you meet with me this afternoon and tell me what this all about?

"Sure, doll, happy to. Let's make it at 4:00. Donatella paid me some major dinero to get the goods on those two guys. I'll bring my report with me. Gotta sign off now. Got a hot little chick in the other room who wants me to get the goods on her husband. Thinks he's seein' some blonde bimbo stripper who works in a ber-le-q on the south side of town, but lookin' at her, he'd have to be crazy to be lookin' fer it elsewhere. See ya' later."

Donatella and this guy? From what I've heard about Donatella I would have thought she would have hired the most sophisticated private investigator available. Well, I've got other things to do at the moment, like get the receipts in the safe now that I have the right combination.

She walked back to the kitchen. "Nico, Sophie, these new dishes have turned out to be so successful I'm going to order permanent new menus from Hank. How many do you think I should get?"

"Ask Carlotta. She's probably a better judge of that than either one of us," Nico said.

"By the way, Kelly," Sophie said, "I just made Nico the chef of Mangia! Mangia! He's going to make a decision in the next day or two about who he wants to have as his sous chef. I think people will automatically assume he is the chef after they eat the new dishes. Just decided to beat them to it."

"I couldn't agree more with your decision. Nico, congratulations. You deserve it."

"Thanks. I feel like I've stepped into some type of a surreal world. Sophie, I haven't even had a chance to tell you. While you were in the office a little while ago, I had a call from Mitch Ramos. He wants to talk to me about possibly starring in a cooking show for his television station. Please pinch me and tell me all of this is really happening."

That's exactly what Tina predicted was going to happen, Kelly thought. *Wonder if Chef DuBois knows?*

"By the way, Nico, I scheduled an interview for you with the television station at 10:00 tomorrow morning here at the restaurant. Did you set up a time to meet with Mitch?"

"Yes, he's going to come to the restaurant tonight around 9:30. I told him I could probably take some time to talk to him because it usually slows way down by then, particularly on a weeknight."

"That's great. I'll be curious to see what happens. Have you ever thought about doing a television show?"

"In my dreams! Like I said, I need to be pinched and have

someone tell me I'm not dreaming. He's even come up with a name for the show – The Best of Chef Bassi. What do you think?"

"I like it. Okay, I'll ask Carlotta how many menus I should order, and then we're off to Hanks's. I'll be back shortly. Rebel, come."

On their way to Hank's, Rebel stopped at the dog park and looked pleadingly at Kelly. "Sorry, boy. Not this time. I've got a lot to do today, and Hank's Print Shop is a high priority. Please try not to make me feel so guilty."

As if he understood her, he nuzzled her knee and started walking towards Hank's. When Kelly opened the door of the print shop, she stood and spent several minutes once again admiring the art on the walls and the beautiful rugs on the floors. A few minutes later Hank walked out from the back room.

"Good afternoon, Kelly. There's quite a buzz going on in the district about the new menu being served at Mangia! Mangia! and the sous chef, Nico."

"Actually he was just promoted to chef based on the reports we got from the diners who sampled his debut dishes at lunch. It's was quite exciting. Who knows? We may just be able to pull this off and save Donatella's restaurant. Don't you think that will be wonderful?"

Kelly noticed that Hank seemed somewhat nervous and was avoiding eye contact with her. He kept shifting his weight from one foot to the other while she was speaking to him. "Hank, is something wrong? Your body language is telling me you don't quite seem like the man I talked to yesterday."

He looked up, took a deep breath, and began to speak. "Kelly, I don't like to speak ill of the dead, and I've been struggling with whether or not I should tell you something, but there are a couple of things I think you need to know. Why don't you have a seat on the couch? I'll get us some iced tea, and we can talk."

Kelly sat down on the brown suede couch, thinking that this had to be the only print shop in the world that had a suede couch in the reception area. A moment later, Hank walked back into the room with two glasses of iced tea.

"Hank, you certainly have a good eye for decorating. I told you this yesterday, but this reception area really is one of the most beautiful I've ever seen."

"Thanks. Not too many people know I majored in art in college, but I just didn't have the fire in my belly to make it in the art world. I guess you could say I'm compensating by surrounding myself with art."

"Actually, it seems to me the printing business and the things you design are a form of art, maybe just not what you had in mind years ago."

"I'd never thought about it like that. You may be right."

"So what do you want to talk to me about? You've really aroused my curiosity."

"Like I said, I really don't like to speak ill of the dead, but Donatella was not quite the person the paper and some of her fans might think she was. She and I had a good relationship, as I told you yesterday, but over time I learned she had a controlling dark side she kept hidden from most people. Let me tell you a little story."

"I'm all ears. Please, tell me everything. The more I learn the more I can help Sophie make a go of the restaurant."

"As you probably know by now, those of us who live and work in the Pearl District are part of a pretty tight knit community. We all try to watch out for each other and help each other's businesses. Donatella didn't like to play that way. About a year ago a young Mexican couple moved here from Tucson and opened a gourmet taco shop a few doors down the street. It was take-out food only, and there wasn't any seating. They were two of the nicest people I've ever met and were so proud of their little shop. In a short time it became quite popular – kind of a 'go-to' place for the shop owners and people who wanted a really authentic taco. They specialized in seafood and fish tacos and they were delicious. Many people who are on the go all the time don't want to spend the time or the money to eat in a restaurant, so lots of people started eating there.

"Everything was fine for the first couple of months, but when the shop became more and more popular Donatella became obsessed with the thought that it was providing unwanted competition for her restaurant. It really wasn't competition for Mangia! Mangia!, it was simply a little upscale taco shop where you could get a quick bite to eat. Donatella hired a private investigator and found out the husband was in the United States illegally. She threatened to go to the immigration authorities if they didn't close the shop and leave town. She told them she would pay them some money, a great deal of money given their limited resources, if they would close the shop. The reason I know this is the young couple and I had become friends. One day they unexpectedly came to say goodbye to me. I couldn't understand why they would close the shop and leave, because it was really doing well. That's when they told me about Donatella's threat. I told them there was nothing I could do to help them, but I remember them saying that Donatella was giving them a large financial gift. Personally, I'd call it blackmail or a bribe, not a gift."

"Yes, you're right, Hank. That's a side of Donatella I haven't heard about. What happened?"

"They took the money, closed the shop, and moved back to Tucson. They were from families who were very poor, and I'm sure the money was a big help to them. I get an email from them once in a while, but that's it. The whole experience left a bitter taste in my mouth. I don't think Donatella ever knew that I knew why they'd closed their taco shop. She told everyone that they hadn't been able to make it because Mangia! Mangia! was so much better."

Kelly sat back on the couch. "Wow! That's about one of the saddest stories I've ever heard. What are they doing now?"

"In their last email Maria told me she was a waitress in a Mexican restaurant, and her husband was working there as a dishwasher. So much for the American dream."

She was silent for several minutes, lost in thought. "Hank, why did you decide to tell me about the young couple?"

"I called the restaurant this morning and spoke with Sophie. As you know, I've worked with her several times when she's hosted dinner parties in her home. I wanted to wish her good luck with the new menu. She told me you were visiting and had agreed to stay on for a few days after Donatella's murder. She said you had been successful in solving several murder cases in Cedar Bay, and that she had asked you to see if you could find out who murdered Donatella."

"Yes, but since the young couple is now in Tucson, clearly, they aren't suspects."

He got up and walked over to the window where he stood silently for several long moments, and then in a halting voice he said, "There's someone else who hated Donatella."

CHAPTER NINETEEN

Hank continued to stare out the window at the never-ending line of people walking by his shop. Finally, after several minutes he turned towards Kelly and said, "I do the menus for all of the restaurants in the district and know all of the people in the local restaurant business. Are you aware of the long-standing feud between Chef DuBois and Donatella?"

"I didn't know there was a feud," Kelly said. "I heard that he wanted to have a television cooking show and was not happy when Donatella was chosen instead of him."

"That's just the tip of the iceberg when it comes to the reasons for the feud. It goes quite a ways back. As fate would have it, they both opened their restaurants here in the Pearl District about the same time. Donatella opened a high-end Italian restaurant, Mangia! Mangia!, and Chef DuBois opened a high-end French restaurant, Le Toque. He told people he was French and had trained extensively as a French chef, although I have some doubts about that."

"I don't understand what you mean. He is the owner of Le Toque, correct?"

"Yes, but that's not what I'm referring to. Mind you, I have nothing to base this on, but I've often wondered if he really is French. I spent a year backpacking around Europe after I finished college. I didn't know what I was going to do with my life. A lot of young people were doing the same thing at the time, and it appealed to me. Anyway, I fell in love with France and the French people. I have a very good ear for languages, and soon I was speaking French like I'd been born there and lived there all my life. I've heard Chef DuBois speak French, and I've noticed that the accents he puts on certain words are completely wrong. I've often wondered if he learned French from some computer online course, like the Rosetta Stone, or some such thing. I know that sounds really farfetched, but something doesn't ring true with him."

"I don't know if you're right about that, but my built-in smarmy detector or woman's intuition or whatever you want to call it, went on high alert when I met him for the first time last night. I thought the way he made a big show of kissing my hand was a little over the top, but then again I've never been around a French chef."

"The restaurant people don't like him. One day he sent one of his kitchen staff over to my shop to pick up some new menus I'd prepared for Le Toque. The young man and I got to talking about what it's like to work in a kitchen of a busy high-end restaurant like Le Toque. He said something that has always stayed with me. He told me Chef DuBois was so angry when one of the vegetable deliverymen brought the wrong order he threatened him with his chef's knife. The young man went on to tell me that while the chef was all smiles to customers, he was always yelling at the staff and had a horrible temper. The staff was terrified of him."

"I hate to hear something like that. I consider the people who work in my coffee shop to be my friends."

"I think acting superior to others and not treating them with respect says more about the person who's in charge than the people who are being yelled at," Hank said. "Kind of like when you see a mother keep hitting her kid in the supermarket. It's the mother who can't keep her temper in check. The kid is just being a kid."

"I couldn't agree more, but back to Donatella and Chef DuBois."

"Sorry, I got a little sidetracked. Chef DuBois always wanted to be the top chef in the Pearl District, but there was one chef who was just as important as he was, if not more so, Donatella DeLuca. She had developed quite a following from the cookbooks she'd written and the various charities she supported. She might have been more likeable than Chef DuBois, but in her own way she was just as ruthless. She too wanted to be known as the top chef in the Pearl District, and Chef DuBois was a constant thorn in her side. The two of them acted like spoiled little brats at times, even going as far as hiring the other's kitchen or wait staffs. It was pretty ridiculous. One time Donatella tried to get me to tip her off if Chef DuBois was going to change his menu, and if so, what he had added or deleted. She even offered me $500 if I'd give her advance notice of any menu changes he was planning. I told her that would be unethical and turned her down."

"Surely this district is big enough to support two high-end restaurants. I find this jockeying back and forth to see who could be number one ridiculous."

"So do I, but here's the final thing about Donatella you ought to know. I don't think Donatella was really in love with Mitch. I think she seduced him, and he fell for it. He left his wife and got divorced shortly after meeting Donatella and, although I have nothing to base it on, I'd bet she did it so she could get her own television show. That would assure her of being the reigning top chef in the Pearl District. I've also heard that Mitch was having financial problems at the television station. He may have divorced his wife for Donatella, but the main reason may have been that he needed Donatella to star in a television show and make him financially healthy."

"So essentially you're saying you think there's a good chance Mitch and Donatella used each other for financial gain, and it was a loveless relationship."

"When you put it like that, yes. Donatella was certainly capable of it. I don't know Mitch all that well, but I'd bet I'm right. I know Chef DuBois really wanted a television show of his own, and he was terribly angry when he found out Mitch decided to have Donatella star in it instead of him. Don't forget there are a few others who disliked her enough to murder her. I've done a lot of work for Elena Wright, much like what I've done for Sophie such as printing menus or invitations for their dinner parties. She never forgave Donatella for the scallop incident. I'm sure you heard about that."

"Yes, although it seemed pretty innocent to me."

"Not to Elena. She blamed Donatella for taking away the one thing she prided herself on being – queen of the dinner parties. Actually, that incident and Elena's response to it made her a laughingstock in the district. Everyone heard about it, and to my knowledge, she never forgave Donatella."

"So, in your opinion, both Chef DuBois and Elena would each have had a motive to kill Donatella."

"Yes. There were even rumors that Donatella wanted to discredit Elena because of her reputation as the foremost dinner hostess in the district. Donatella not only wanted to have the best restaurant in the district, but she wanted to be the top food person in all respects. I've heard some people say she took a deliberate gamble that someone from the Midwest who had never had scallops might have a food allergy to them, and that's why she served scallops. Seems a bit far-fetched to me, but who knows? Things aren't always what they look like on the surface."

"Wow! You've given me a lot to think about. Hank, bear with me, but I'd like to take this conversation in a whole different direction if you'll indulge me for a moment. It seems to me you and Sophie have an awfully lot in common, such as your love of France, art, and food. I may be overstepping my bounds, but have you ever thought of seeing her socially as a woman rather than simply providing printing services for her?"

He was quiet for what seemed like an eternity to Kelly, and then he began to slowly speak. Choosing his words carefully he said, "I met Sophie when she was married. They entertained a lot, and I did the menus for their dinner parties. I never liked her husband. I was happy when they got divorced, and she renovated the warehouse building and moved closer to my shop. She's a wonderful woman, and we've had some great conversations about art and food. I never told her I'd spent some time in France."

"Why?"

"She was married to a very rich man. I'm not a rich man. She worked in a fashion house. I was backpacking around Europe. We're from different worlds. I've never approached her about being anything other than a customer, because I don't think I could stand to be rebuffed by her. I suppose I'd rather continue to get a few crumbs rather than risk trying to see if I could get a full loaf of bread. What prompted you to ask about Sophie and me?"

"I don't know. I do know she's rather lonely, and I just have a sense that perhaps you might care for her. For whatever its worth, she does speak very highly of you. You know, Hank, when we get to be our age sometimes it's important to take risks, because we don't have a lot of time to wait for things to happen. I think if you asked Sophie to dinner or coffee or whatever, she would be receptive. Why don't you try it?"

"Do you really think a wealthy, sophisticated, and yes, classy woman like her would ever be interested in a short, grey-haired print shop owner? Get serious!"

"A man who speaks French fluently, is knowledgeable about art, and a man who knows everyone in the restaurant world in the Pearl District? Yes, I think she'd be very interested. I believe you have much more in common with each other than you may realize. I hope when I get back to Cedar Bay I get a call from Sophie telling me she's going to be sharing a fabulous bottle of wine with you."

"Tell you what, Kelly. If that happens, I'll call you! And thanks for the suggestion. I need to think about it."

"It's time for me to go. I have a murder to solve and a dog and husband to get back to in Cedar Bay. I really appreciate your stepping up to the plate and telling me about the things we just discussed. Thanks for your honesty. See you later. Rebel, come."

CHAPTER TWENTY

Kelly left Hank's Print Shop in a hurry, realizing she was just going to make it back to the restaurant in time for her appointment with Dirk, the private investigator who had done some work for Donatella. She opened the door and saw a thin man wearing a dark blue suit that had seen too many trips to the cleaners with a grey fedora plopped on the back of his head seated in the reception area. Carlotta smiled at her and said, "Mrs. Reynolds, Mr. Lewis is here to see you, and your husband would like you to call him when you have time."

"Thanks, Carlotta." She turned to the man and extended her hand. "Hello, Mr. Lewis, I'm Kelly Reynolds. It's nice to meet you. Let's go back to my office where we can talk. Please follow me."

He stood up and doffed his hat towards Carlotta. "Nice talkin' to ya' doll. Remember, ya' need anything, jes' call me. Ya' got my card." He followed Rebel and Kelly down the hall to her office.

"Please have a seat, Mr. Lewis. May I get you some coffee or water?"

"Nah, but I see ya' got a fully stocked bar out front. I'd take a jack black."

"Certainly, but I don't know what that is."

"Fer' someone runnin' a restaurant ya' don't know much. It's Jack Daniels with dark rum and coke. Goes down real easy."

Kelly called the bar. "Would you please bring me a Jack Daniels with dark rum and coke? I have a guest who would like one."

"Sure, Mrs. Reynolds. We call it a jack black."

"Thanks," she said, feeling like an idiot and from the look Dirk Lewis was giving her, it was obvious he was thinking the same thing.

He opened up the battered briefcase he carried, took out some papers, and handed them to her. "Here's the report I gave Donatella. You can read it, or I can tell you the guts of it."

She stood up and answered the knock on the door. "Thank you, Jimmy," she said to the young waiter. She handed Dirk the jack black. "Why don't you tell me what you found out? I can read the report later when I have a little more time."

"Thanks, doll. It's half-past thirsty time. Need a little somethin' to wet my whistle, and jack black always does a good job. Okay, I investigated two men for Donatella. That food critic from the Portland Gazette and the chef from Le Toque."

"I've met both of them," Kelly said.

"Then ya' ain't gonna be too surprised at what I'm gonna tell you."

"That remains to be seen. Let's get started."

"I'm gonna start with the food critic, guy who goes by the name of Bill Hossam. Dude was born David Smith in Garden City, Kansas. Seems he was hot to get outta Kansas, like who wouldn't be, so he attends, and I use the word loosely, the Cordon Bleu in New York. You'll notice I said 'attends.' Dude was expelled from the school for plagiarizin' recipes. Evidently he was takin' a class that required the students to come up with original recipes in a bunch of different categories. Some other dude in his class discovered a Garden City church cookbook in his desk with a number of recipes circled in red. Turns out he used those recipes and claimed they were original recipes made up by him."

"What a disgusting individual. I sensed there was something about him. Can't say I'm all that surprised," Kelly said.

"That's not all, doll. Dude left New York and went to Chicago and opened a restaurant. This part's a little hazy, but it seems there mighta' been some sorta' Mafia connection, but I couldn't nail it. Did find out there were a number of silent partners in his restaurant. Dude made the mistake of embezzlin' funds from them. Looks like he hotfooted it outta there, changed his name, and convinced a couple of small papers in Oregon to hire him as their food critic. Dude had a gift for food writin' and eventually was hired by the big kahuna here in Oregon, the Portland Gazette."

"So am I to understand you told Donatella all of this?"

"Ya' got that right. Met with her and gave her the goods on him. It's all in that there little ol' report. Other dude I investigated for Ms. Donatella was Chef DuBois. Now if he ain't jes' a real piece of work."

"What do you mean?"

"Dude's about as French as the Chinaman that owns that little hole-in-the-wall laundry down the street. He was born Lenny Jones in some backwater town in Georgia. Family was poor as church mice. He quit school when he was ten and started workin' in restaurants to put some food on the table. Had a whole mess of rug rat brothers and sisters he had to help feed. Word is he stole as much food as he prepared. He bounced from one place to another. Got to give him some credit though, dude had some smarts. Took a bunch of on-line French courses and decided to reinvent himself as some fancy schmancy Frenchie. A few months later he's callin' himself Pierre DuBois and speakin' French. Gets himself a job at some French restaurant in Atlanta.

"Guess the dames liked him, cuz he was able to marry three rich broads. Too bad one always died before he married the next one. He helped himself plenty to the money these rich dames gave him. Dude got enuf' bucks he was able to come out here to Portland and open his restaurant, Le Toque. Name seems a little silly to me. I was curious what it meant, so I looked it up on-line. It means the tall white hat the chef wears. Dude has some nerve considerin' he never even went to chef school. 'Bout as mucha' chef as I am," he said as he tossed back the last of his black jack and set the empty glass on Kelly's desk with a flourish. She ignored his obvious effort to try and cadge another free drink from her.

"Someone else told me they didn't think he was French because when he pronounced certain French words he put the accent in the wrong place," Kelly said. "That sort of goes with what you just told me. He's a totally fake Frenchman. Right?"

"Absolutely, and it really ain't no surprise given what I found out about him. So the dude's got this fancy French restaurant, and he's tellin' everyone he should have a television program like some of the other chefs. Donatella had a gut sense there was somethin' off with the guy, so she hired me to check him out, and my investigation proved just how right she was."

"Dirk, do you think she went to either of these men and told them what she knew about them?"

"Don't know for sure, doll, but I'll tell you this. Lady liked to have people think of her as the queen bee of the Pearl District, but jes' between you and me don't think she was better than either one of the two phonies described in my report. I think she had a dark side to her that her friends and the public never knew about."

"Why do you say that?"

"Had a meetin' with her last week and tol' her all this stuff. All of a sudden it seemed like she completely forgot I was in the room cuz she kinda starts talkin' to herself and says somethin' like 'Okay boys, I'm getting both the show and the rave review or else the world is gonna know all about you two.' Then she got real quiet, thanked me, and handed me a check fer' my services. Last I saw of her."

"I'm getting the feeling you didn't like her very much."

"Think she'd been eatin' at the same table as them 'ol boys had. Maybe even drank the Kool-Aid if ya' know what I mean. Ya' know the old sayin' about 'honor among thieves.' Dead wrong in this case. None of these three thieves had an ounce of honor in 'em, her included."

"Wow! It's rather apparent you don't think much of her."

"Ya' can take that to the bank."

"This may seem like a strange question, Dirk, but I'm curious why she hired you and not some investigator from a blue chip Portland firm. After all, the way you dress, talk, and even drink on the job doesn't really promote your downtown image."

"Doll, whatever Donatella was, she was smart. I was recommended to her by someone I'd done some work for. She understood when ya' talk like the people on the street and ya' look like the people on the street, ya' get a lot more information from the people on the street than ya' would if ya' told them ya' went to Oregon University Law School and graduated at the top of your class. People tend to not trust those types."

"Are you telling me you're a law school graduate?"

"Ain't many people know it, but that I am, doll, that I am. Even got me a license to practice law, but I like what I'm doin', plus I make more money doin' this than I would practicin' law." He uncrossed his long legs and stood up. "Time to get back to the salt mine. Thanks for the jack black and if ya' ever need a private eye, I'm 'Dirk the Jerk, the One with a Gun.' Har har!" He handed her his business card and gave her a mock half-salute as he walked out of the office. She sat in her chair for several minutes, stunned at what he had told her about Hossam and DuBois, but even more stunned to learn who

Dirk really was.

Sitting there, her thoughts turned to what Dirk had said about Donatella. *I wonder if Dirk's impression of Donatella is correct. Was she really a scheming, conniving business woman who would stop at nothing, including blackmail, to keep her restaurant in the top spot in the district?*

CHAPTER TWENTY-ONE

A few minutes after Dirk had left, while Kelly was giving Rebel a fresh bowl of water, she began to think about whether or not it had been a good decision to bring Rebel to the restaurant. *I know having a dog in the restaurant could be an issue, particularly for that food critic if he ever found out, but I can't believe anyone would have a problem with Rebel being in the office. If push comes to shove, I can always defend having him here by saying he never was near the food preparation area, but hopefully it won't come to that.*

She picked up her cell phone and called Mike. "Hi, sweetheart. What's up?"

"How about if you tell me first? Did the new additions to the menu go over well?"

"Mike, it was the most unbelievable thing." She told him about the customers lined up at the door, the diner's responses to the dishes, how Nico had been made chef, and was even being considered for a television show.

"Sounds like you've had a busy day."

"I have. There's so much to do here, and I know I don't have much time. However, I'm not sure I'm any closer to solving the murder today than I was when I talked to you last night."

"Well, I have a little something for you on that issue. I spent some time this morning researching a couple of the names you gave me last night. Nico Bassi studied at the Cordon Bleu in Portland and attained an associate degree in their culinary arts program. He's the real deal as far as credentials go."

"Well, he's got more credentials than Chef DuBois or Bill Hossam."

"What are you talking about?"

"I'll tell you when you finish."

"Okay, back to where I was with Nico. I also checked out his personal background. His parents were divorced when he was very young. Evidently his father left his mother, and Nico never saw him again. His mother worked two jobs to support them, and his grandmother practically raised him."

"That doesn't surprise me. He told us some of his recipes had come from his grandmother and how proud she'd be of him."

Mike continued, "He has no history of arrests or any other problems with the law. He's clean. That doesn't mean he didn't commit murder for the reasons we've already discussed, but there's nothing that makes him stand out as a suspect."

"Thanks so much, Mike. I like him, and I'd hate to think he did it. I know he would have had a strong motive – to be the chef at Mangia! Mangia!, the head person in the kitchen, not the sous chef, the second in command. And I can't forget he'll probably be widely acclaimed for his new dishes that are on the menu, something that never would have happened as long as Donatella owned the restaurant. Find out anything else?"

"Yes. Elena Wright seems to have some major psychological issues. She spent a lot of time in a private mental institution out of state. Her father is a very wealthy lumber baron and didn't want anyone to know about it, so he paid for her to be admitted to a very expensive private facility in Washington, near Seattle."

"Were you able to find out why she was admitted to the facility?"

"Yeah, it took a little doing, but it looks like she suffers from a mental condition everyone's heard of, delusions of grandeur. I was able to talk to the doctor who treated her at the facility, and he told me that when she entered the facility she believed she was the most famous hostess in the United States."

"What kind of therapy do you use for something like that?" Kelly asked, sitting back in her chair and doodling on a notepad.

"He told me it usually is part of a larger psychological issue, such as the person being bipolar or even having substance abuse issues. There didn't seem to be a history of substance abuse, but he did put her on the same medication he uses to treat bipolar patients. He said she didn't have a lot of the symptoms of someone who classically suffers from the disease, but her mother had been bipolar and there are different degrees of it. He seemed to think the medicine helped her."

"Given that kind of medical background, I suppose she very well might have felt terribly threatened by the scallop incident. In other words, as the French would say, her 'raison d'être,' which means the thing that was most important to her, was ruined because of Donatella, or at least that's how she possibly saw it. I suppose in her mind that could have been reason enough for her to want to kill Donatella. I've even heard rumors that Donatella wanted to discredit Elena because of her reputation as the foremost dinner hostess in the district. Donatella wanted to be the top food person in all respects. I also heard a rumor that she took a gamble that someone from the Midwest who had never had scallops might have a food allergy to them, and that's why she served scallops. Seems a bit far-fetched, Machiavellian if you will, but who knows? Things aren't always what they look like on the surface." Kelly said.

"No, they're not."

"Did you find out when she was in the private mental facility?"

"I asked the doctor that very question, and he said it was five years ago. I suppose it's possible she could have stopped taking her medication or that her mental situation has taken a turn for the worse. There's no way to tell without a battery of tests being done on her."

"If it turns out she's the one who did it, I imagine the court would insist on a full mental fitness evaluation. I don't know if you found out anything about Tina Ramos, but let me tell you about a visit I had from her this afternoon."

"Yes, I researched Tina, but I'd like to hear what you have to say first."

Kelly told him about the surprise visit she'd received from Tina and the one hundred eighty degree turn she'd made between yesterday and today. "Honest, Mike, it was like I was talking to a completely different woman."

"Well, it may seem like that, but she still had a very good motive for killing Donatella. From what my research showed, she has a long history of alcohol abuse. She's had three DUI's and even spent some time in an alcohol rehab center as part of her court sentence. As a matter of fact, the entire family has a long history of it. She inherited quite a sum of money from her parents when they died in an auto accident after they'd been drinking heavily at a bar in Portland and ran off the road on their way home. Her brother died a few years ago of cirrhosis of the liver, so even though she says she's never going to have another drink, I'm not so sure she's to be believed. Sounds more to me like a classic morning after thing to say."

"Wow! To come from a family like that and then have your husband leave you for another woman. That's kind of sad."

"Don't go getting all soft on me. It's not a good characteristic to have when you're investigating a murder case. Believe me, I speak from experience. Just keep in mind that she very well may be the person who did it."

"I suppose you're right. Mike, you won't believe the meeting I just had with a private investigator who told me all about Bill Hossam and Chef DuBois." She told him everything Dirk had told her and the strange difference between his education and how he chose to earn a living.

"First of all, I'm not surprised that he acts and talks like that. He's absolutely right, if people think you're on their level or below it, they'll tell you a lot more than if you come off as highly educated. It's probably a pretty good strategy in his line or work. As for the chef and Hossam. They both jump to the top of my list of possible suspects. They both had an awful lot to lose if Donatella ever blew the whistle on them."

"I wonder if she threatened the chef. Remember, Carlotta said she'd overheard Donatella threatening Hossam. Maybe she was going to go to the Gazette and blow the whistle on him. That would certainly give him a reason to murder her. I agree with you. I'd put him pretty high up on the list of suspects.'

"I've got to go. I'm running late for a meeting. I'll call you later. Don't forget we have a deal. You, the gun, and Rebel. Deal?"

"Deal, Sheriff. Love you."

"Bye, babe. Be safe."

CHAPTER TWENTY-TWO

Kelly had just ended her call to Mike when the office phone rang. "This is Kelly."

"It's Carlotta. I don't know what to do. We don't open until 5:30 for dinner, and not only is every table reserved tonight, there must be twenty people standing in line outside the restaurant. I can't believe it. It makes the lunch line look like nothing. I can't figure out how everyone heard about the new dishes. One of the people said they saw something on television, and someone else said they read about the restaurant in an article that was in the Gazette. We must be all over the media, but I've been too busy to look at the television or turn on the radio. Plus, I just got a call from that restaurant critic, Bill Hossam, and he made a reservation for four people for tonight. I don't know how I'll do it, but I was pretty sure you'd want me to work him in."

"Absolutely. Thanks, Carlotta. Give me a couple of minutes, and I'll come out and help you. Let's do it this way. We'll give the people with reservations first priority, and if we have any open seats we'll plug in the others as best we can. Since they don't have reservations, I really don't think there's anything else we can do, and they'll just have to understand. It's also kind of a reverse psychology kind of thing. The more you can't have something, the more you want it. Try and get as many people as you can into the bar area. I know that's where the restaurant makes the most profit. See if you can call in another bartender for tonight. If this continues, we're definitely going to have to hire more people. I'll go alert the kitchen."

She gave Rebel his evening meal which he ate with his usual vigor. "Between what's happening at the restaurant and trying to solve Donatella's murder, I'll really be glad to get back to sleepy Cedar Bay. How about you, big guy?"

He wagged his tail and looked up at her. She could swear he was sending her a message that he wasn't a big city dog, and he couldn't wait to get back to Mike and Lady. "Okay, you stay here and guard the receipts, while I do battle in the restaurant. See you in a couple of hours."

She walked into the kitchen where Nico and Sophie were huddled in the corner going over the food that needed to be ordered within the hour for delivery the next morning. "Whatever you're ordering, I'd suggest you double it." Kelly said.

"What are you talking about?" Sophie asked in her soft French accented voice.

She told them about the call she'd just received from Carlotta. "It looks like tonight's going to be busier than we were at noon, and tomorrow's going to probably be even busier. I know we can only serve a certain number of dishes, but what worries me is that they're going to start placing orders to take out, and we should be ready to fill those as well. Nico, if you need to call in some more kitchen help, feel free to do it. I'm going to work with Carlotta in the front of the restaurant. Call me if you need me."

Kelly walked into the dining area of the restaurant just as Carlotta unlocked the doors at 5:30. By 5:40 there wasn't an open seat at any of the tables and it was standing room only, and not that much of it, in the bar.

"I called several waitresses and waiters to help us out tonight," Carlotta said." We should be fine for tonight, but we definitely need to hire more people. A number of people waiting in line have decided to place orders to go instead of waiting for a table, if one even opens up, so I have one of the wait staff assigned to take care of the to go orders."

"Good thinking. That's been a concern of mine."

"Kelly, I know you're new in town, but everyone who is anyone in the Pearl District either has made a reservation for tonight or is presently standing in line. I can't believe what I'm seeing."

Kelly looked at her watch and realized an hour and a half had already gone by. She'd made two trips to the office to put the receipts from the bar and the reception desk in the floor safe. Each time she admonished Rebel to be on guard. She looked outside when she returned to the reception desk the second time and saw that even more people were standing in line.

This must be every restaurant owner's dream, but in some ways it's becoming a nightmare. I'm ready for this night to be over.

Much later, after the night had finally ended, she'd look back and remember that innocent thought.

CHAPTER TWENTY-THREE

Kelly stood behind the reception desk while Carlotta showed the diners to their tables and gave them the old and new menus. While she was looking at the seating chart and wondering if any more diners could be accommodated, she heard a voice say, "Good evening, Mrs. Reynolds." She looked up and was face to face with the restaurant critic from the Portland Gazette, Bill Hossam.

"Hello, Mr. Hossam. It's good to see you, but I must say I'm surprised. I thought you weren't going to come back for a week."

"I've been getting calls all afternoon about the changes here in the menu at Mangia! Mangia!, and I thought I better see what all the buzz is about before it dies down. You know you can't possibly expect to maintain this," he said haughtily as he gestured at the full restaurant.

"Good evening, Mr. Hossam," Carlotta said, "Do you wish to be seated now, or do you want to wait for the rest of your party?"

"Seat me now. The other members of my group texted me they're running a little late."

Kelly noticed he didn't bother to thank Carlotta or show her any other courtesy. *Obviously he feels he's superior to her. One of the things I hate more than anything else in the world – people who think they're better than everyone else and don't even need to acknowledge those they consider to be lesser than them. Yeah, Mr. Hossam, but I know the truth about you, Mr. Big Shot. I'm tempted to blackmail you myself, but I suppose that wouldn't go over very well with a certain sheriff I happen to be married to. I'll just have to keep my mouth shut and grin and bear it.*

A few minutes later she said, "Carlotta, I'm going over to Mr. Hossam's table for a few minutes. I need to talk to him."

"Sure. I can handle it. The line outside is down to a trickle, but we sure did a huge take-out business. I wonder how close the kitchen is to running out of ingredients for the new dishes."

"I have no idea. The only time I left the front desk area of the restaurant was to take receipts back to the office. I have no way of knowing what the previous best night's receipts were for the restaurant and bar, but whatever they were, I bet we've already broken that record tonight. We still have a couple of hours to go, and from the looks of the bar crowd, some of them might be around until closing time, meaning even more profits."

"Kelly, I don't know about you, but I'm bone tired. My face hurts from smiling, and if I had a penny for every time I've explained what is in the new dishes on the menu, I'd be a rich woman. And I know darned well the diners probably asked the wait staff the same thing! Go and enjoy Mr. Big Shot Food Critic. Too bad Donatella didn't serve him some of her infamous scallops."

"I wish I could say I didn't agree with you, Carlotta, but I do. He really is a pompous arrogant so-and-so. If it wasn't for Sophie and the restaurant, I could easily do without ever having anything to do with that man. I'll be back in a few minutes."

She walked over to his table and sat down across from him. When he was finished reading the messages on his cell phone, he looked up at her. "What can I do for you?" he asked.

"I'm curious how someone gets to be a food critic. We don't have any where I come from, just people who like good food. How did you wind up in this kind of a job?"

"Well, I started out in New York at the Cordon Bleu. After I graduated from there, I decided I'd rather help people find good places to eat than cook for them. The profession has been very good to me. I have one of the best reputations of any food critic in the entire United States. I've been told I should think about going to Italy or France, but I never perfected those languages. The only things I know about either one of those countries are the dishes that come from there. A lot of people say that my talent is wasted in a city as small as Portland, but I must admit I like the Northwest."

"Well, you certainly have a following. What about San Francisco or Los Angeles?"

"I don't like people from California. They're so into whatever the newest fad is. Once you've spent time at the Cordon Bleu and been with really great chefs, you realize there's far more to cooking than theatrics. Every restaurant I've ever been to in California seemed to rely more on some chef's ability to do what they call 'molecular gastronomy,' which is just a fancy word for using all kinds of things like making gas bubbles taste like chocolate rather than preparing food in the classical manner. You know, the kind of food like I had to prepare when I was a student at the Cordon Bleu. And don't even get me started on those chefs who are so hot on the 'sous vide' method of cooking. That's just vacuum packed food cooked in a warm bath at a low temperature. In my mind, those two methods of cooking are examples of theatrics at its worst."

"I have to admit I've not tasted anything cooked in either one of those methods, but I sure have been seeing a lot about them in the food magazines and on the television food shows."

"Oh those people don't know anything. That's why my column is so important and popular. People want to know what someone trained at the Cordon Bleu thinks of a restaurant rather than have some gorgeous hunk or beauty queen who doesn't know a turnip from a piece of tuna tell them what the latest is in molecular gastronomy or sous vide cooking."

"I see your point. If I may change the subject, are you originally from New York? I don't detect a New York accent."

"Yes. I lived and worked at restaurants in New York until I came out here. Several people urged me to come to Oregon because it was obvious to them that the Northwest needed a food critic of my caliber. My parents were originally from the Midwest, so that's probably why I don't have an accent."

"I see Carlotta escorting some people to your table. Your guests must have arrived. I hope you enjoy the new additions to our menu. The other diners speak very highly of them."

"For your sake, I hope I do too."

That certainly sounded like a veiled threat if I ever heard one. What an officious horrible liar. I wouldn't put it past him to be the one who murdered Donatella. Anyone who thinks that highly of himself would no doubt do whatever was necessary to make sure no one ever found out the truth about them. Should have told him that just like Dorothy in The Wizard of Oz, he wasn't in Kansas anymore or maybe better yet, tell him to click his heels three times and say there's no place like home and I think I'll mosey on down the road back to Garden City. Too bad Donatella didn't have a bad scallop day at the restaurant or at least arrange for one particular diner to be the recipient of one of them!

CHAPTER TWENTY-FOUR

"Kelly, there's a call for you on line two," Carlotta said. "Do you want to take it here or in the office?"

"As loud as it in here, I better take it in the office. Do you know who's calling?"

"Yes. He said it was Detective Masters."

"Good. I've been wondering why I haven't heard from him. Please tell him I'll be with him in just a minute."

She walked down the hall and into the office, looking over at the rear door that led to the alley to make sure it was double locked. Even though she'd carefully put all of the receipts for the evening in the floor safe, it still made her nervous that there was a separate entrance into the office. Carlotta had told her that Donatella didn't want the staff to know when she wasn't on the premises, so she had a door cut into the wall which gave her direct access to the alley. That way she could come and go whenever she wanted, and the staff would never know when she was gone.

Probably makes a lot of sense, but it makes me nervous. Maybe that comes from being married to a sheriff. I know some of the things that can happen, and often they're not always pleasant.

Rebel walked over to her as she sat at the desk and put his paw on her lap. Kelly knew that was his way of letting her know he needed a little reassurance. "It's okay, Rebel. We'll be going home in just a couple of days. One way or the other, whether I solve this murder or not, we're going back to Cedar Bay, and it can't be soon enough for me. Maybe it's time I told Detective Masters everything I know and let him solve the murder. That's what he's being paid for."

She picked up the phone. "Good evening, Detective. How are you?"

"One hundred percent better than I've been the last couple of days. Sorry I haven't called, but I've really been sick. I caught some kind of a flu bug from my kids and the bathroom and I have been best friends ever since I last saw you. I finally felt well enough to come into the office this evening only to find out there's been a rash of homicides in the area, so nothing has been done on the DeLuca murder case. Makes me crazy, because one of the basic things we're taught is the first twenty-four hours are the most important in solving a case like this. The chances of ever solving it go down every hour after that. So I'm way behind the eight ball on this one."

"I'm glad you're feeling better. I have to admit I was kind of surprised when I hadn't heard from you, but maybe I can help you. I've found out a few things I think you need to know. I wish I could stay and help you on this case, but I have a feeling I need to get back to Cedar Bay. Do you have a few minutes?"

"Of course. What have you got for me?"

She spent the next half hour telling him everything she'd found out, who she felt the suspects were, what Mike had found out about Elena and Tina, about Nico's background, and ended by relating her conversation with Dirk about the investigation he had conducted at Donatella's request of Chef DuBois and Bill Hossam. When she was finished, there was a long silence on the other end of the line.

"Mrs. Reynolds, do you have a background in law or police investigative work?"

"No, but my husband is the sheriff of Beaver County, and I've been able to help him solve a couple of cases. That's one of the reasons that Sophie, the new owner of Mangia! Mangia!, wanted me to stay for a few extra days."

"Your husband's a very lucky man to have you help him, if what you've told me about this case is any indication."

"I don't think he'd agree with you. He would prefer it if I never got involved in any of his cases again, and he certainly wasn't happy about my involvement in this one, but things kind of happened, and for better or worse, here I am. As a matter of fact he made me promise I'd keep Rebel, my ninety-five pound boxer, and my gun with me at all times."

"Seems to me you've done a heck of a job identifying the suspects. Let me see if I can sum it up. I believe you've told me about five people who might have had reason to murder Donatella. At this time I don't think there's enough evidence on any of them to make an arrest. I suppose what I need to do now is see if they have alibis for where they were between ten and midnight the night she was murdered. The coroner's report said Mrs. DeLuca was murdered during that time frame."

"That would sound right. I remember when we found her she was wearing the same dress she'd worn to the dinner party, and she left Mrs. Marchant's home about 9:30 after the dinner party."

"The lab report indicated that Donatella's fingerprints were the only ones on the knife. Evidently it was her own chef's knife, but if Nico did it, it probably could have come from the restaurant, however I'm more inclined to believe it was from her home."

"I agree. The morning we found her Sophie mentioned she thought she'd seen that knife on a previous occasion in Donatella's kitchen. Looks like maybe someone wanted to show the irony of a chef being murdered with a chef's knife."

"Thanks for all your help, Mrs. Reynolds. It would have taken me days to do what you've done in a period of just two short days. Now I need to figure out what to do next. Do me a favor and give me a call before you leave town, and would you let Mrs. Marchant know I'll probably be visiting the restaurant in the next day or so? By the way, tell your husband I agree with him. I definitely think you should keep that big boxer and your gun with you. If you were my wife, it would be the first thing I'd tell you to do."

"Thanks, Detective. I feel like a weight has been lifted from my shoulders. I'm glad I could help you."

"By the way, I hear the restaurant is really doing well and there are some killer new dishes on the menu. Tell Mrs. Marchant I'll probably schedule my visit around lunchtime, so I can try them."

Kelly laughed. "I'll tell her to reserve a special place for you, but you better call first. If today was any indication, there won't be any walk-in seating for a long time. I'd hope it would hold true for the foreseeable future, but the public being as fickle as it is, that probably won't happen. Good night, Detective."

CHAPTER TWENTY-FIVE

After finishing up with Detective Masters, Kelly returned to the front of the restaurant. There still wasn't an empty table in the dining area, and from the loud voices coming from the bar, she knew the bartenders would shortly have to start refusing service to a few of the customers. She looked over at the table where Bill Hossam and his party had been. There was no sign of him, and it looked like the table had been reset to accommodate new diners.

Will this day and night never end? I agree with Carlotta. I've never been so tired!

She glanced at her watch and saw that it was already 9:30. *Enough. I need to prepare the deposit for the pickup tomorrow morning by the armored car service and do some other paperwork. I probably won't get out of here for at least another hour. Wonder how the kitchen staff is holding up.*

Kelly walked to the back of the bar. The bartender handed her a leather pouch with more receipts for the evening. She picked up a similar one from the reception desk. "Carlotta, I need to do some paperwork in the office. It looks like that's the last of the seating. I just glanced out the window next to the front door, and I didn't see a line, so I think the worst is over for tonight. I'd appreciate it if you could come in about half an hour early tomorrow. You, Sophie, Nico, and I need to decide what we're going to do about staffing. See you in the morning."

She took the pouches back to the office and put them in the floor safe, then she walked to the kitchen. "Nico, where's Sophie? I wanted to tell her that Carlotta, you, Sophie, and I need to have a meeting tomorrow morning about staffing. We may have to start without you if you're tied up with that television interview."

"Sophie was exhausted, so I told her to go home about half an hour ago. I think she personally chopped a hundred pounds of vegetables. The staff usually does all the chopping, but it was all they could do to get out the new dishes in a timely manner. I honestly don't know what I would have done without her."

"How are you and the staff holding up?"

"We're all tired. Mitch is scheduled to be here in a few minutes to talk to me about the television show, but it's so noisy here in the kitchen I think I'll have to meet with him in the alley, right outside the back door to the kitchen. If you hear voices while you're working in your office, it will just be us."

"Good luck. I'm off to figure out how the restaurant did today and prepare some checks for Sophie to sign for the vendors, as well as paychecks for the staff. Donatella kept a big file on both, so I should be able to figure it out."

"See you later. I'll let you know what happens about the show after I talk to Mitch. Keep your fingers crossed."

"Will do."

I just remembered I promised Mike I'd call him tonight and knowing him, he'll be frantic if I don't. Better get that out of the way before I do anything else.

"Hi Mike. Sorry to call so late, but it's really been a zoo around here. I can't remember being this tired, but I have some good news. Detective Masters called. He's been really sick and off work for the last couple of days, and that's why he hasn't called. I wondered why I hadn't heard from him. He was very frustrated that nothing had been done on the case while he was gone. Evidently there were several other homicides in Portland, and since he was out sick, no one worked on the DeLuca murder case. I'm ready to come back home to Cedar Bay, so I told him everything I knew. I hope you don't mind, but it doesn't make any sense for me to stay here any longer."

"Are you kidding? That's the first thing you've said in a long time that I totally agree with. Believe me, Lady and I will be more than happy to have you back home."

"Sorry, Mike, I didn't hear you. I've got to go. I hear a lot of yelling going on in the alley outside my office door, and I've got to check it out."

Rebel heard the noise too and was already standing by the rear door that led to the alley, hackles raised, growling, and looking at Kelly as she reached for her gun and threw open the door leading to the alley.

Chef Pierre DuBois was standing in the alley with a wide-eyed half-crazed look on his face. He was holding a small pistol in his hand. The big dog acted from instinct. No command was needed or given. The moment the door swung open he instantly assessed the situation and lunged at Chef DuBois, biting the lower pant leg of his black and white checked chef's pants and forcing him to stagger backwards, nearly knocking him to the ground. At almost the same moment Hank appeared out of nowhere, wrapped one arm around Pierre's throat, and with his other hand, knocked the pistol out of his hand.

"Get him off, get him off of me! I hate dogs! Get him off!" Pierre yelled.

Kelly trained her gun on Pierre. "Chef, you've got a lot of explaining to do. If you don't answer my questions, I'll tell the dog to attack, and I promise you he'll tear your leg off before he's finished with you. Do I make myself clear?"

Everyone started talking at once. "Nico and I were just standing here in the alley talking and he…" Mitch said. "He said he was going to kill me," Nico said in a halting voice with fear written all over his face. "Get the dog off…" Pierre screamed.

"Everyone be quiet. Rebel, on guard! Chef, I'm not releasing him until everyone has had a chance to talk."

"Kelly," Mitch said, "the chef walked up to us, and I never suspected a thing was wrong until I saw the gun in his hand. I asked him what was going on. He told me he was going to kill Nico just like he killed Donatella. He said if he couldn't have the television show, no one else was going to have it."

Nico interrupted, "It was like something out of a scary movie. He was talking like a totally deranged person and in a voice with no trace of a French accent about how he'd always hated Donatella and her restaurant. He said one of the staff here at Mangia! Mangia! had called him and tipped him off that Mitch and I were meeting in the alley, and that it was a good thing he paid some of my staff to keep him informed."

"Chef, answer this question or the dog will do whatever it wants to you. Believe me, if I give the attack command, you won't live to see tomorrow. Did you kill Donatella DeLuca?"

"Get the dog off, he's about ready to bite me! I can feel his teeth on my leg. Get him off me. Please! I'll tell you what you want, just get him off of me."

"I think I asked you a question. I'd like the answer."

"Yes. I killed her," the chef said in a high-pitched quivering voice. "She threatened to tell everyone I wasn't French, and then on top of that she got the television show. Yes, I did it, and she deserved it. She was a cruel, mean, conniving woman who was always out to get me."

"Rebel, stand down. Hank, why in the world are you here? I don't understand."

Hank had released the choke hold he had on Pierre but was

carefully watching every move that Pierre made, which wasn't much with Rebel standing just inches from him and staring at him in an obviously agitated state. He looked over at Kelly and said, "I live above my print shop, which as you know is just a few doors down the street from Mangia! Mangia! Every night I do some breathing exercises and open the window that looks out over the alley. I noticed someone wearing white and sneaking down the alley, trying to stay in the shadows. I realized it was Chef DuBois in his white jacket walking towards Mangia! Mangia!

"I saw something glinting in his hand and thought it looked like a gun. I don't think I even had a rational thought after that, I just reacted. I was afraid something bad was going to happen to Sophie. I ran down the stairs and into the alley. I've had a lot of martial arts training, and I can follow almost anyone without them knowing I'm right behind them. I followed him and listened to him scream at Nico that he was going to kill him. I was afraid if he sensed I was behind him, he would fire the gun out of a reflex action and kill Nico or Mitch. Fortunately your dog attacked when you threw open the door, and it provided an opening for me to get my arm around his neck and make him drop the gun he had in his hand."

Kelly and the men were suddenly aware of police cars coming towards them from both ends of the alley. Within seconds, Detective Masters was standing next to Kelly. "Kelly, I'll take over. I assume this is Chef DuBois," he said, motioning toward the chef who was wearing his chef's uniform. "Since you've got your gun pointed at him, my guess is that you may have just made my life a little easier by solving the DeLuca murder case. Might I be right?"

"Yes, you're absolutely correct. He just admitted he killed Donatella, and he was going to kill Nico. We all heard him say it." Rebel stood next to Kelly, still growling. She put her hand on his head, letting him know she wasn't in danger. He stopped growling but backed up against her leg as close as he could get.

Detective Masters looked at Chef DuBois and said, "Chef, where you're going you won't need those fancy checked pants, so that big piece missing out of the bottom of your pant leg isn't going to be a big deal. Kelly, I've worked with police dogs for years, and it looks like a dog took a large bite out of the chef's pants. Did your dog do that?"

"Yes, that's right, but you told me you weren't going to come to the restaurant for a day or two. Why did you show up now, and why did you come to the alley?"

"That sheriff you're married to called me as soon as you hung up on him. He asked me to check on you and said you heard yelling coming from the alley. I was on my way to Le Toque to talk to Chef DuBois anyway, so I was very close. From the looks of things, seems like you handled everything on your own." He turned to Mitch, Nico, and Hank. "I need to take a statement from each of you. Give me a minute, and I'll get back to you."

He directed two of the policemen who were with him to handcuff the chef. After he was handcuffed they put Chef DuBois in the back seat of the police car, and it pulled away.

"They're taking him to the station and booking him for murder and attempted murder. I see a lot of people working in the kitchen. Is there somewhere other than in the alley where I can talk to all of you?"

"Let's go into the office. It's quieter there and we'll have some privacy. We still have a lot of diners and people at the bar in the front of the restaurant, so I don't want to take you in there," Kelly said

Forty-five minutes later Detective Masters closed his notebook and said, "Sounds like you've told me everything. I'm sure you're all exhausted after a day like today. Go home and get some sleep. I have your contact information if I need to speak further with you and thanks for all your help. I need to go to the station and make a report, but if you think of anything else, give me a call."

"Nico, I'll call you tomorrow about the show. Think about the offer and see if it's something you'd like to do," Mitch said as he walked out of the office and down the hall to the front of the restaurant where the valet had parked his car.

"Are you all right, Nico? I can't think of a more stressful day," Kelly asked.

"I'm fine, but I sure want to find out who called Chef DuBois and told him Mitch was here. I told the staff I was meeting him in the alley, because it was too noisy in the kitchen. I have no idea who did it, but it darn near cost me my life. Make no mistake, that person will be gone by tomorrow."

"I understand, but you might want to wait a day. This has to be one of the most grueling days you've ever spent, and that's something you might be able to put off."

"Don't think so," he said grimly as he walked out the door in the direction of the kitchen.

CHAPTER TWENTY-SIX

After the meeting with Detective Masters had ended, Kelly, Rebel, and Hank walked out of the office. "Kelly, let me walk you home. I know you've got that big guy with you, but I'd feel better knowing you and Sophie are safe in the house with the alarm system on and the dogs in there with you," Hank said, looking worried.

"After everything's that's happened tonight, I'm not going to turn down your offer. Thanks," she said in a shaky voice.

They crossed the street to Sophie's home and Kelly knocked on the door. Sophie opened it, obviously having recently gotten out of the shower. A towel was wrapped around her head, and she wore a thick white terry cloth robe.

"Hank, what are you doing here at this hour?"

He looked at Kelly. "Do you want to tell her or should I?" Hank asked.

"I will. Better sit down, Sophie. This might take a while."

She told Sophie everything that had happened from the time Detective Masters had called her to when he'd left to go to the station and write up his report on Chef DuBois. "Hank is a hero. He risked his own life to save Nico's life. He was worried something might happen to you when he saw the chef in the alley headed towards your restaurant. I thought you should know."

"*Mon Dieu*," Sophie said as she walked over to Hank and kissed him lightly on the cheek. "Thank you so much. I don't know the English words to even begin to tell you what I'm feeling. If it hadn't been for you, who knows what would have happened. How can I ever thank you?"

"How about saying you'll have dinner with me at your restaurant?"

She laughed. "*Chéri*, I would love to, and I can even promise you that I can provide a good bottle of champagne to go with it!"

Hank opened the door and turned to Kelly. "I think that dog's a keeper. Sure made my job easier. Might want to think about giving him a little treat. Night ladies."

"Sophie, we can talk tomorrow morning," Kelly said. "Right now what we both need is sleep, but first I've got to call Mike. He's probably frantic by now."

"I agree. Sleep well."

*****

"Thank heavens, you called. Are you all right?" Mike practically shouted into the phone when she called.

"Yes, Rebel and I are fine. It's over, Mike, and I'm very glad you thought to call Detective Masters. Here's what happened." She spent the next few minutes telling him about the chef, Hank, Nico, Mitch and finally the heroics performed by Rebel. "Mike, I'd love to talk longer to you, but I'm so tired I'm going to start babbling if I continue. I've got to get some sleep. I love you, and I'll be home early tomorrow afternoon. I have to attend my last meeting at the restaurant tomorrow morning and then I'll head for home."

"Tell you what, I'll make dinner and get a nice bottle of wine. It's been beautiful here so there's a good chance we can eat on the patio. Deal?"

"Yes, sweetheart, that's a deal."

CHAPTER TWENTY-SEVEN

The following morning, after the meeting about increasing the staff had ended, Sophie and Kelly walked back to Sophie's building to get Kelly's luggage and say goodbye.

"I never like goodbyes, Sophie. I much prefer to say, I hope I'll see you soon, and I'd like to do just that. Please keep in touch. I'm really interested in hearing about the success of the restaurant and also about you and Hank."

"Aah, *chérie*, who knows? I'll call you in a few days and tell you what's happening in the district. If you don't like goodbyes, you probably don't like to be thanked, either, but I can't let you leave without thanking you and telling you how much I appreciate everything you've done for me. Without you, my new chef and I very well could have been the next victims of Chef DuBois. Listen to me, using words like 'my new chef.' It all seems so very strange, but for me life is just an adventure from one day to the next. Drive safely, and I definitely will be calling you. *Au revoir.*"

"Okay, Rebel, say goodbye to Amelie. We're off to Cedar Bay."

She put her bag in the back of the minivan and opened the door for Rebel. As she drove away from Sophie's building, she saw Sophie waving until she turned the corner. Two hours later she pulled into the driveway of her home in Cedar Bay, the home that had been her parents until they retired and moved to Arizona. She sat in the van and was caught up in a moment of reverie as she looked at the bay shimmering in the early afternoon sunlight.

A moment later the door to the house burst open, and Mike and Lady ran over to the minivan. As soon as she opened the door she was enveloped in a huge bear hug from the burly sheriff. Lady gave her own greeting to Rebel, gently poking at him with her nose as if to say, "Missed you, big guy. Glad you're home. It was lonesome here without you."

A few hours later, Rebel woke up, looked at Lady and then down the hall to the closed bedroom door as if to say, "We need to tell them to get up from their nap. It's time for them to feed us."

*****

Several days later Kelly had just locked the door at Kelly's Koffee Shop and was walking to her car in the pier parking lot when her cell phone rang. She looked at the screen and saw the name Sophie Marchant.

"Sophie, how are you? How is Mangia! Mangia!? How is everything in the Pearl District?"

"*Chérie*, stop," Sophie said laughing. "I can only answer one question at a time. I'll start with the restaurant. Nico found out who called Chef DuBois and tipped him off about the meeting in the alley between Mitch and him. It was one of the line cooks, and he fired him on the spot. We've hired five new people for the kitchen and seven people for the wait staff. One of them does nothing but handle take-out orders. Believe it or not, we are still as busy as we were when you were here. Actually, we are booked solid for the next few weeks for lunch and dinner. We'll open up the reservations again in a few weeks or so. Can you believe it?"

"After tasting Nico's amazing dishes, I'm not the least bit surprised. Donatella sure made a bad business decision by not allowing him to put his dishes on her menu."

"As to how the Pearl District is doing, it's fine," Sophie continued. "What's interesting is that this morning there was a rave review in the Portland Gazette by Bill Hossam on Mangia! Mangia! After you told me what you found out about him, I'm surprised he can pull off these reviews, but a rave review by him is pretty much gold for a restaurant. Don't you Americans have some saying about how you can fool someone?"

"Yes, and he's probably a good example of the saying which is 'You can fool all the people some of the time, and some of the people all the time, but you cannot fool all the people all the time.' Actually it was one of our presidents who said it, Abraham Lincoln. I had to write a paper on it in a high school history class, and I've never forgotten it. Sure seems to apply to him, but I still think someday he'll write a nasty review for a restaurant, and the owner will have him investigated and then everyone will know what a fraud he is. I'm so glad he gave the restaurant a rave review. That's fantastic!"

"Detective Masters called me the other day to tell me there's more than enough evidence to convict Chef DuBois if his case goes to trial. His restaurant, Le Toque, is closed, and I don't know what will happen to it. The detective said his restaurant staff hated the chef and was terrified of him. Evidently he was physically abusive to some of them and emotionally abusive to all of them. Several of them have come to Mangia! Mangia! looking for work. The detective said the chef was hoping some of his staff would testify in his behalf. I guess he expected them to serve as character witnesses for him, but none of them would."

"Couldn't happen to a better person," Kelly said. "Can't say I feel too sorry for him."

"I don't either. I'm saving the best for last."

"Well, I hope it's about you and Hank."

"It is. I've seen him several times since you left Portland. I like him, Kelly, I like him a lot. We'd talked a little bit about art and food before, but now it seems like there's never enough time to talk about everything we have in common. He told me I have you to thank for that. He said he never would have had the courage to approach me if it hadn't been for you, so I guess that's one more thing I have to thank you for. Actually, I pretty much have my life to thank you for, so thank you."

"I just happened to be in the right place at the right time. My mother always used to tell me to bloom where you're planted," Kelly said, "and I guess I was planted in the Pearl District and bloomed for you. Maybe that's a stretch, but you know what I mean."

"I do, dear friend. I see Nico motioning to me, so I better see what the next kitchen crisis is all about. Thank you again. I'll be in touch."

"Give everyone my best, and tell them Rebel and I will come to visit sometime soon."

"*Au revoir.*"

Kelly ended the call and smiled peacefully to herself.

Who doesn't love a happy ending, she thought, *and this is about the best ending anyone could ask for.*

EPILOGUE

One evening a few weeks after Kelly returned to Cedar Bay, she and Mike were just finishing dinner when her cell phone rang. She looked at the screen and didn't recognize the number displayed on it.

"Hello, this is Kelly Reynolds," she said.

"Well, hello there yerself' lil' ol' Ms. Kelly," a stranger said in an obvious slurred tone of voice. "This here's yer' ol' buddy Dirk the Jerk. You member' me doncha'? Did that little ol' report for Donatella DeLuca concernin' those two scumballs she wanted me to get the goods on. You know, that phony French chef and that food critic guy that was threatnin' to give her restaurant a bad name."

"Yes of course Dirk, I remember you. How are you doing tonight? Sounds like maybe you've been drinking a little, or, if I'm guessing right, maybe a lot, given the sound of your voice. What can I do for you, Dirk?"

"Well yer' right on target about me having a little too much to drink. Got my ol' friend jack black right here on the table in front of me. Jus' got through making m'self a brimmer, ya' know, all the way to the top of the glass and no ice. Goes down real smooth like, 'specially when you're in the mood to do some serious celebratin'.

"Anyway, the reason I'm calling ya' is I was jes' wonderin' if you

129

subscribe to the Portland Gazette, cuz if ya' do, you otta' take a gander at the lead article that's gonna' be in the paper's weekly food section tomorrow mornin'. Got's me an inside contact at the paper, and she tipped me off 'bout what's gonna be in it."

"What are you talking about?" Kelly asked.

"Seems like the editor of the paper hisself is gonna 'nounce that he's fired their longtime food critic, Bill Hossam, and he's gonna' make a public 'pology fer' allowin' Hossam to work for the paper under false pretenses. 'Cording to the editor, turns out Hossam was a complete phony and had zilch credenshuls or qualific' whatever the word is."

"I think you mean qualifications."

"Yep, jes' like I was sayin'. He ain't got no qualific' to be writn' weekly articles 'bout restaurants for the Gazette. My friend at the paper said she didn't know how the editor found out about Mr. Phony Baloney Hossam, but she did say there was a rumor circulatin' in the newsroom that the editor got some kinda' 'nonymous report in the mail about his star food critic, good ol' Mr. Hossam. Imagin' that! Wonder who in the world mighta' done somethin' nasty like that and gone and spilled the beans on him? Heh, heh, that's a rich one!

"Well anyway, Ms. Kelly, thought you'd wanna' know. Have a good night tonight and don't forget to take a look at the Gazette in the mornin'. As for me, think I'll have me one more little ol' taste of honey, my ol' pal jack black. Nitey-nite," he said and hung up before Kelly could say a word.

Well, I can't say I feel sorry for Hossam. He was an evil disgusting man and it looks like he's going to get what he deserves. I guess the old saying "What goes around comes around," certainly applies to the situation in which Bill Hossam now finds himself!

*****

Later that evening, after Kelly had told Mike about the phone call and Bill Hossam being fired by the Gazette and exposed as a fraud, he said, "Kelly, remember how we talked about taking a real honeymoon after Jesse's murder was solved?"

"Sure, but it just never happened. Between your cases, Kelley's Koffee Shop, and then the murder in the Pearl District, we've never had time. Why?"

"I think it's time we did it. We could both use some time off. I received a call from my Aunt Agnes this afternoon. You may remember me telling you about her. She is my mother's sister, and when I was a kid I spent a lot of time with her during the summers at her home in Calico Gold, California. She and her husband never had children, and I think I was kind of their surrogate child. The little town is really something. I've got great memories of it. It's nestled in the foothills of the Sierra Nevada Mountains in Central California. There's quite a little bit of history about the part it played in the Gold Rush."

"Mike, didn't you tell me once your aunt owned a big house on a large ranch."

"Yes, her house is on one hundred acres outside of town. When she and my uncle were younger, they had horses, dogs, cats, goats, and all kinds of animals. Believe me it was a little boy's paradise. I used to ramble around that big old house and think it must be just about the biggest one in the world. Now that I'm a lot bigger and a lot older, it probably wouldn't seem that big."

"What did she have to say?"

"It was kind of interesting. She asked if there was any way you and I could visit her as soon as we could. She couldn't make it to our wedding, and she'd like to meet you. She said something that was rather cryptic and makes me think I should pay her a visit as soon as possible. She mentioned that maybe I could use some of the skills I've learned as a sheriff to help her with a problem she was having. Her husband, my Uncle Jim, passed away nearly twenty years ago, and ever since then she's lived the life of a lonely widow in that big old house."

"Did she say what the problem was?"

"No. As I said, it was rather cryptic. Anyway, I thought maybe you and I could drive over there with the dogs and pay her a visit. We could stay for a few days and sort of treat it as a delayed honeymoon. I feel I owe her for all the wonderful times I spent there as a child, and if she's in trouble, I would never forgive myself if I didn't go. How does it sound to you if we take a trip down there?"

"Wonderful. I could use some time off from work. From the number of times you've mentioned her and the property, I know she's very dear to you. I agree, you'll never forgive yourself if you don't go. Consider it done. Why don't' you call her as soon as we figure out when we can go. I'll call Roxie right now and see if she can cover for me at the coffee shop while we're gone. She seemed pretty happy with the extra money I paid her when I went to Portland. She mentioned she and her husband could really use it, so I'm sure she'll be happy to do it. Why don't you check your schedule and see when you can take off? If it's a go for both of us, I can be ready day after tomorrow."

"Lady, you never fail to amaze me. You've never even met Aunt Agnes, and you're ready to drop everything and see if we can help her. No wonder I love you so much."

"Never could say 'no' to a man in a sheriff's uniform," she said laughing. "Calico Gold here we come!"

RECIPES

CHEF NICO'S LASAGNA (For the Home Cook)

Meat Sauce Ingredients

1 pound Italian sausage (mild flavor)
½ pound ground beef
1 box mushrooms, roughly chopped
1 tsp. salt
½ tbsp. ground pepper
1 tbsp. dry Italian seasoning
¼ tsp. red pepper flakes
6 cups marinara sauce (you can use prepared type in jar, about 1 ½ jars)
2 tbsp. water, more as necessary

Ricotta Cheese Mixture & Pasta Ingredients

2 eggs
2 lbs. ricotta cheese
8 oz. shredded mozzarella cheese
2/3 cup grated parmesan cheese
1 tsp. salt plus salt for pasta water
¼ tsp. ground pepper
Pinch cayenne pepper
16 oz. pkg. lasagna noodles
8 oz. diced mozzarella cheese (for topping at end of assembly)

½ cup grated parmesan cheese (for topping at end of assembly)

Meat Sauce Directions

Over medium heat cook sausage and ground beef in large frying pan until brown and crumbly. Cook mushrooms in separate small frying pan until they give off water and add to meat sauce. Add salt, pepper, Italian seasoning, and red pepper flakes. Add marinara sauce and water to meat mixture. Reduce heat to low and simmer about 1 hour. Add more water as necessary if mixture becomes too thick. Using a small spoon, skim excess fat off surface of mixture.

Ricotta Cheese Mixture and Pasta Directions

Preheat oven to 375 degrees. In large bowl, beat eggs. Stir in ricotta cheese, 8 oz. shredded mozzarella cheese, and 2/3 cup parmesan cheese. Add salt, pepper, and cayenne pepper. Set aside.

In pasta pan or large pan bring salted water to boil (should be about as salty as ocean water.) Boil lasagna noodles for approximately 15-20 minutes. Noodles are done when firm to the bite. Drain and immediately place in a bowl of ice cold water to stop the cooking.

Assembly of Lasagna Directions:

Use a 10" x 15" Pyrex baking dish.

Preliminary Note: There will be 3 layers of noodles. Lay 1st layer longways in the dish, the 2nd layer crossways, and the 3rd layer longways. Remove noodles from cold water, dry off, and place in dish as directed below. Best to count the number of noodles available for assembly and divide by 3 so you don't run out of noodles when you get to the last layer!

Assembly: (1) Spread ¼ of meat sauce in bottom of dish. (2) Top with 1/3 of noodles (longways). (3) Spread ½ of ricotta cheese mixture over noodles. (4) Spread ¼ meat sauce over ricotta cheese mixture. (5) Top with 1/3 of noodles (crossways). (6) Spread remaining ½ ricotta cheese mixture over the noodles. (7) Spread ¼ meat sauce over ricotta cheese mixture. (8) Spread last 1/3 noodles (longways) over meat sauce. (9) Spread remaining ¼ meat sauce over noodles. (10) Sprinkle meat sauce with 8 oz. diced mozzarella cheese and ½ cup grated parmesan cheese.

Cover assembled casserole with aluminum foil and place on cookie sheet to catch any spills. Bake 30 minutes. Remove foil and continue to bake until top is golden brown and bubbling, about 30–35 minutes. Remove from oven and let rest for 15-20 minutes before cutting into squares and serving. Enjoy!

NICO'S SEAFOOD BUCATINI (For the Home Cook)

Ingredients

2 lbs. Manila clams
16 oz. bag frozen seafood mixture (you can usually get this in the frozen section of the supermarket); usually contains scallops, mussels, small shrimp, etc.
6 large precooked shrimp, tail on
2 cups marinara sauce
6 garlic cloves, diced
3 large green onions, diced (bulb portion only)
1 med. onion, diced
1 tbsp. red pepper flakes
1 tbsp. saffron threads (I know they're expensive, but they keep forever!)
1 tsp. fresh thyme, chopped
2 tbsp. olive oil
3 cups white wine
2 tbsp. chopped parsley for garnish
1 box bucatini pasta
Water for pasta and clams

Directions

Sauce: Sauté diced garlic 3 minutes in olive oil in large frying pan over medium heat. Add diced onion and cook 3 minutes. Add diced green onion and cook one minute. Add 1 cup white wine, red pepper flakes, thyme and saffron, seafood mixture, and large shrimp. Combine gently and cook until shrimp turn pink. Add marinara sauce and stir. You can add wine as needed to keep sauce from becoming too thick. Keep warm in pan until ready to serve.

Pasta and Clams: Bring water to boil in pasta pot or other large pot. Boil pasta for about 20 minutes. When noodles are firm to the bite, strain and set aside.

When pasta is approaching the end of cooking time, bring 1 cup of wine and 1 cup of water to a boil in medium size pot. Add clams. Cover and cook 3-4 minutes, steaming them. Remove clams from heat when shells open. Throw away unopened ones (they may be bad, don't eat them). Drain clams and set aside while still in the shell.

Note: Drain and set aside clams before you drain pasta.

Place drained pasta in empty pan used to cook clams. Pour sauce over the pasta, add the clams, and toss gently to coat.

Serve on large family style serving dish. Garnish with chopped parsley. Enjoy!

FROZEN KEY LIME PIE

Crust Ingredients

1 ½ cups graham cracker crumbs
¼ cup sugar
6 tbsp. melted butter (3/4 of stick)

Filling Ingredients

6 large egg yolks
¼ cup sugar

14 oz. can condensed milk
2 tbsp. grated lime zest
¾ cup fresh lime juice

Topping Ingredients

1 cup sour cream
2 tbsp. powdered sugar
1 tbsp. lime zest (garnish)
2 tbsp. lightly toasted slivered almonds for garnish

Directions

Preheat oven to 350 degrees. Using a large whisk, combine graham cracker crumbs, sugar, and melted butter in bowl. When combined, press into 9" Pyrex glass pie pan. Bake 10 minutes or until golden brown. Cool completely. Beat egg yolks and sugar at high speed for five minutes. If using a countertop mixer, use the paddle attachment. Reduce speed to medium and add condensed milk, lime zest, and lime juice. Mix for 1-2 minutes. Pour into baked pie shell and freeze.

After filling is frozen (about 2 hours) remove from freezer. Combine sour cream and powdered sugar. Spoon mixture on top of frozen filling, smoothing and leveling. Sprinkle with lime zest for garnish. Return to freezer (1 hour) or until ready to serve. To make it easier to cut into serving pieces, remove from freezer for approximately 20 minutes before serving or until slightly softened. Sprinkle top with almonds for additional garnish. Serve and enjoy!

COQ AU VIN (CHICKEN IN WINE)

Ingredients

1 tbsp. olive oil
4 oz. Applewood bacon
3 to 4 lb. chicken thighs and breasts
2 tsp. kosher salt

1 tsp. freshly ground pepper
½ lb. carrots, cut diagonally into 1" pieces
Yellow onion, sliced into 6-8 pieces
3 cloves garlic, chopped
½ bottle (375 ml) dry red wine such as cabernet or burgundy
1 cup chicken stock
10 fresh thyme sprigs (leaves only)
2 tbsp. unsalted butter at room temperature
1 ½ tbsp. all-purpose flour
½ pound frozen small whole onions
½ lb. brown mushrooms, stems removed and quartered
2 tbsp. chopped fresh parsley

Directions

Preheat oven to 250 degrees. Heat the olive oil in a large Dutch oven pot. Add bacon and cook over medium heat for 8-10 minutes, until browned. Remove bacon to a paper towel covered plate and when cool, crumble.

Pat chicken dry with paper towels. Sprinkle both sides with salt and pepper. Brown chicken pieces in batches in a single layer in bacon fat, about 5 minutes, turning to brown evenly. Remove chicken to the bacon plate and continue to brown all the chicken pieces.

Add carrots, yellow onion, salt, and pepper to pan and cook over medium heat for 10-12 minutes until onions are lightly browned. Add garlic and cook 1 minute. Add bacon, chicken, wine, chicken stock, and thyme to pot and bring to a simmer. Cover the pot and place in the oven for 30-40 minutes, until chicken is no longer pink. Remove from oven and place on top of stove.

Mash 1 tablespoon of the butter and the flour together. Stir into chicken mixture. Add frozen onions. In medium sauté pan, add remaining 1 tablespoon butter and cook mushrooms over medium low heat for 5-10 minutes until browned. Add to chicken mixture. Bring to a simmer and cook for another 10 minutes. Serve in individual bowls and garnish with chpped parsley. It's also good served over mashed potatoes or rice. Enjoy!

CARAMEL SAUCE FOR ICE CREAM

Ingredients

2 tbsp. butter
¾ cup brown sugar
1/3 cup light corn syrup
3/8 cup evaporated milk

Directions

Put butter, brown sugar, and corn syrup in saucepan and bring to a boil over medium heat until it reaches the soft ball stage (drop a small amount into a cup of water and when it forms a soft ball on its own, it's ready). Remove from heat and slowly add evaporated milk. It thickens as it cools. Will save in refrigerator in a covered container for quite some time. Serve over vanilla ice cream. Enjoy!

ABOUT THE AUTHOR

Dianne lives in Huntington Beach, California with her husband Tom, a former California State Senator, and her boxer puppy, Kelly. Her passions are cooking and dogs, so whenever she has a little free time, you can find her in the kitchen or in the back yard throwing a ball for Kelly. She is a frequent contributor to the Huffington Post.

Her other award winning books include:

Cedar Bay Cozy Mystery Series
Kelly's Koffee Shop
Murder at Jade Cove
White Cloud Retreat
Marriage and Murder

Liz Lucas Cozy Mystery Series
Murder in Cottage #6

Coyote Series
Blue Coyote Motel
Coyote in Provence
Cornered Coyote

Website: www.dianneharman.com
Blog: www.dianneharman.com/blog
Email: dianne@dianneharman.com

Printed by Amazon Italia Logistica S.r.l.
Torrazza Piemonte (TO), Italy

13582362R00084